In my bedroom Tom and Topaz began laying out on the bed various garments from their collection and from my own closet, which Topaz knew as well as his own. Their briefcase was filled with cosmetics, perfume bottles, and jewelry.

"First, your undergarments," said Tom, "for they are the foundation on which our entire impression must rest. Undergarments are to the human form what primer is to the canvas of a potential masterpiece."

"Which is what you are," said Topaz.

"This human masterpiece does not wear panty hose," I said.

"Why not?" said Topaz.

"Have you ever worn pantyhose!" I demanded.

They both stifled a snort of laughter.

"Never mind," I said. "I'll do it." I took off my sweater and folded it on the bed. Then I unbuckled my overalls; the bib dropped suddenly, dumping onto the floor pencils, tools, change, and a tape measure. "Shit," I said, getting the pant legs stuck on my shoes, which I had forgotten to take off. "After all," I said, "how hard can it be? Right?" By now I was lying on my side, kicking my legs and snarling.

SOUTHBOUND

The Sequel to Faultline

BY
SHEILA ORTIZ TAYLOR

The Naiad Press, Inc.
1990

Printed in the United States of America on Acid-free Paper
First Edition

Edited by Katherine V. Forrest
Cover design by Pat Tong and Bonnie Liss
    (Phoenix Graphics)
Typeset by Sandi Stancil

Library of Congress Cataloging-in-Publication Data

Taylor, Sheila Ortiz, 1939—
    Southbound / by Sheila Ortiz Taylor.
        p.   cm.
    ISBN 0-941483-78-9
    I. Title. II. Title: South bound.
PS3570.A9544S66   1990
813'.54--dc20
                                                    90-6099
                                                    CIP

For my daughters Andi and Jess,
with love

I would like to thank Margie Craig for her loving support, for reading and critiquing the manuscript, for our long conversations about imaginary playmates;

my sister, Sandra Ortiz Taylor, for expensive phone calls on the nature of art, death, metamorphosis, and Della Street's relationship with Perry Mason;

Janet Burroway for her theories about why it takes so long to write a novel;

the Meaning of Life Club for its insights, psychological support, and Saturday night dinners;

Janet Heller, for sharing her lore on New Orleans and Newcomb pottery and acts of creation;

Mary Jane Ryals and Joy Lewis for graciously reading the manuscript and offering exquisitely gentle criticism;

Rosemary Catacalos and the Guadalupe Cultural Arts Center of San Antonio for inspiration, a place to write, and a wonderful audience of senior citizens;

Juan Bruce-Novoa, for helping me find my way back to the Chicano community;

Marta Harley, for generous and expert consultation on matters medieval;

Brenda of AAA for planning Arden's trip west;

and the English Department of Florida State University for keeping me in ribbons and paper these last three years.

CONTENTS

BOOK I

1   Great Expectations   3
2   A Nice Girl Like You   8
3   Appliances   18
4   Combination Plate   34
5   Dropping By   40
6   The Tower   50
7   Thanksgiving   62
8   Happy Birthday to You   83
9   Adjustments   90

BOOK II

10   Time's Wingéd Chariot   105
11   Beyond Tupperware   125
12   Touching Down   131
13   Long Distance   136
14   Tamales   143
15   Members of the Cast   146
16   Lunch with Valentine   150
17   Garage Sale   155
18   Who's On First   158
19   Absolution   165
20   Maps   167

BOOK III

21 Wing Dance 173

22 Breaking Bread 184

23 Pressed Flowers 192

24 Mud 203

25 Second Lining 205

26 Bear Facts 216

27 Dead Reckoning 224

BOOK I

CHAPTER 1:
Great Expectations

I was right to have put off employment until the last possible minute. Job hunting is always fraught with danger, leaving aside the whole question of what happens when — Goddess forbid — you actually find adult employment.

School had always seemed a safer place to be. I had always been happy in school. The principals were women then. They let you garden on Wednesdays and called square dances out on the blacktop every other

Friday afternoon. There was the civilized tradition of Nutrition, a thirty-minute period in which you ate sticky buns and calmed your mind. If you colored your maps carefully and learned to read, you were permitted to go your own way and in your own sweet time. Graduate school was not much different. Except that it ended. Unwittingly I had approached a time of termination.

It was Professor Gridley who first mentioned it. The Gridleys of this world, whatever their sex, are the only impediment offered to those of us who would prefer to go to school forever. They view school as a transient state and their task to find your weak spot and jab it at regular intervals to test whether you are worthy of ascending — bearing the standards of the alma mater — into what they are pleased to call "the real world."

Questions of reality have always struck me as largely irrelevant.

One day I was in the English Reading Room re-reading *Jude the Obscure* when I felt Gridley's shadow fall across my book. Possibly I irritated her when I looked up and said, "Sir?"

She crooked her finger at me and turned so quickly her reading glasses swung out on their gold chain like tiny, amusement park airplanes. I followed her rectangular back. By the time I made it through the doorway traffic she was leaning against the hall with her arms crossed. The spot she picked for our *tête à tête* made me a little uneasy; the women's restroom was just opposite and in a moment of weakness I had written an unkind remark about Gridley's favorite Dickens novel inside one of the stalls.

"How old are you, Benbow?"

I nearly said three. Instead I said I was going on thirty-eight, and she smiled her crimped Victorian smile as if I had at long last rewarded her three years of selfless patience with a correct answer.

"Exactly," she said. "It's time you were on your way."

"Where?" I asked.

"Into the real world," she said slowly and distinctly, as if to the hard of hearing. "I take this trouble with you, Benbow, because I think you're worth it."

I tried for a smile of gratitude.

"Of course, you and I both know how I feel about your defection to the Creative Writing Program." She barked an ironic laugh here and paused briefly, hoping for an answering arf. Ungratified in that matter, she gave the jacket of her suit a little professional tug, and assumed the demeanor of one prepared to go it alone. "There was a future for you in Dickens Studies once," she resumed, gazing toward the women's room as if she could see inscribed on the far stall door my insulting remark about Little Dorrit's mental abilities, and beyond that the vision of the scholar's life she had once planned for me, now blighted and stunted. "And how odd," she continued, "how lamentable that the very people who have most need of secure futures seem least interested in securing them." Here she paused so the irony could boomerang into my heedless and ungrateful bosom.

"Let me tell you a little secret, Benbow." Her face softened dangerously. "I once thought of having a child." I almost crossed myself at the thought. "But I

5

came to my senses. As the immortal Bacon once remarked, 'Children are hostages to fortune.' I realized that just in time. The scholar's life must be solitary, free, undomestic. Unless one has a wife, of course." She made that little hamster sound again, and I bit my lip.

"So I simply decided," she continued in a self-congratulatory tone, "that children were a luxury I could not afford. You have six, do you not, Benbow? I like to be sensitive to the presence of other people's hostages to fortune, though I have none myself."

Things were getting labyrinthian. It always makes me nervous when people feel obliged to remind me how many children I have. I glanced significantly at my watch, trying to suggest that one of the hostages to fortune had an orthodontic appointment.

"And that's why I ask you now if you've got your letters out?"

"My letters?"

"Your query letters."

"Query?"

"Your job letters. You are finishing up in the spring, Benbow. Are you not?" Here Gridley made a dumb-show gesture, like an airline attendant identifying the location of emergency exits, oxygen masks, and flotation devices.

"Finishing?"

"You'll need three hundred, minimum. And type each one. That's very important. No copies. Puts them off. You want to create the illusion for each university that you are applying only to them."

"Three hundred?" I said. I knew I had to stop turning her statements into questions, and that unofficially school — for me — was over.

"And tell them that your dissertation is almost complete. Poems, aren't they, Benbow? A slim volume of verse, as I recall?"

"Yes," I said to the woman who had ruined Dickens for me forever.

She made her little hamster sound one more time and headed into the women's restroom, leaving me to my three hundred letters, my hostages to fortune, and my uncertain journey into the obscurities of the real world.

CHAPTER 2:
A Nice Girl Like You

Do you believe in signs and tokens? It was that same afternoon that the Dean of Arts and Sciences had my motorcycle removed from his parking place and impounded. I began to perceive that the universe had revoked my Get Out of Jail Free card and that the cosmic system of debits and credits was about to present its bill for almost five years of remarkable peace and good luck.

After several phone calls I located the Impound

Lot and spoke briefly to an illiterate youth named Lonnie, who said I'd have to come down and pay towing charges. By then it was around four and the campus had quieted down and the sun was growing cool, floating down toward Westwood Village. It was mid-September and the trees were flirting with fall.

Of course most people say Los Angeles doesn't have a fall or a spring and certainly no winter, but they are wrong. Seasons here bear a subtlety and a sense of decorum unknown in more flamboyant climes. They test your acuity.

My feet sought out some leaves to crunch. Then I swerved from my course to walk through the Botanical Gardens where I often ate my lunch. There were winding pebble paths and trees leaning in curious shapes and little signs identifying everything in Latin. It may have been a tad on the controlled side but it was always quiet, and an orderly little stream meandered through it from eight to six every day except Sunday.

I emerged through a stand of banana trees and sighted a corner of what had to be the Impound Lot. Dusty cars stared forlorn through Hurricane fencing topped with a snarl of barbed wire. I expected armed guards but instead saw a sallow youth who had to be named Lonnie trying to make his own escape through the padlocked gate.

"Thought you weren't coming," he said and swung the gate back open in satiric welcome.

I followed him into a stifling metal outbuilding, one of those ironically known as a "temporary." It was dark inside and smelled like small, dead animals. He flipped on a fluorescent light and started a large exhaust fan with blades the size of an airplane's.

Then he sat down at a rusty metal desk and reached for the phone. "Just got to check you out," he said.

"What do you mean, 'check me out?'"

"Prior violations." He had a nose like a collie and little pig eyes with greasy lids. "You'd be surprised how many people try to get away with not paying their parking tickets."

He read off to someone the student ID number I'd given him, letting his dirty eyes drift up a mountain of broken desks, chairs, and book cases in the far corner. Then he snorted through his collie nose and said, "Three hundred and nineteen? Okay, thanks Louise." He hung up and tilted back in his swivel chair, tempting the fates.

"Three hundred and nineteen what?" I asked.

"Dollars," he said, making strangled sounds of amusement. "That's got to be a record."

"That's ridiculous," I said. "It can't possibly be that much."

"Louise says it is."

"Look, Lonnie," I said, trying to look menacing. "I don't have that much money."

"Neither did they," he said, gesturing with his nose toward the imprisoned cars.

"I'll *get* the money, Lonnie."

"You got sixty days before the auction," he said in a happy voice.

It wasn't until he padlocked the gate behind us that I realized I had no way of getting home.

I had to get that motorcycle back. I couldn't write poems without that motorcycle. Why? Because physical movement is a metaphor for mental activity, because travel means knowledge, because death pursues us ever on his black horse, and because I still owed six hundred dollars on it. That's why.

My aunt Vi, who inspired me a dozen years ago to build my first motorcycle out of spare parts left behind by the Youths for Christ one memorable summer in Guaymas, my aunt Vi always said each person must find her own vehicle of inspiration. It had been nearly five years now since I had allowed anyone to tamper with my vehicle. Malthus was the last.

I tend to speak of my ex-husband Malthus as if he were dead. Actually he appears every Saturday to take the children out for dangerous rides and indigestible food. His greatest horror in life seems to be the possibility that one day he'll find himself in a room alone with his six children. He might be obliged to engage them in conversation. Malthus fears silence.

Alice, my life partner, says I rile myself up whenever I begin to catalog Malthus' transgressions. When my memory seems to be taking a dangerous turn Alice will walk up, put her arm around my waist, give a good squeeze, and tell me I'm divorced from him.

But it is hard to get truly divorced if you have children in common. Emergencies will arise. Money must change hands. Visitations — it seems — must happen. Though at several removes, somehow Malthus' opinions continued to flood our house and from time to time drown our spirits. Junk food was not the only offering from Malthus that knotted up in my children's stomachs at night.

By the time Alice picked me up in front of the

Impound Lot I had begun to believe that somehow Malthus was behind the seizure of my vehicle of inspiration.

"But sweet," objected Alice, neatly slipping into second gear, and beaming her aviator sunglasses briefly in my direction, "what can Malthus possibly have to do with your motorcycle?" Alice had come right from work and was wearing a neat little gray linen suit around whose neck the breeze from the window teased her soft gray hair. Alice has small ears that look like seashells anyway, but today each was graced with a tiny abalone shell earring, a sight threatening now to distract me from my rage state.

"Little enough," I growled.

Alice smiled. I never regarded these smiles as tyrannies. They were more like blessings.

"Someone named Louise says I owe three hundred and nineteen dollars for parking violations."

"Surely not," said Alice, with a gratifying gasp of astonishment.

"And if I don't pay it they'll auction off my motorcycle."

"We'll pay it," said Alice, spotting an opening in the dense traffic and heading for it.

"I suppose we can manage," I said.

"There's the money from my promotion," she reminded me. "We've still got six hundred or so from that."

"Alice, my love," I breathed, sinking back into the soft cushions of her aging Volvo, "whatever would I do without you?"

* * * * *

The pain of losing my motorcycle on Monday, however temporary, completely eclipsed my recollection of Gridley's marching orders. Wednesday afternoon I pressed Alice's check for three hundred and nineteen dollars into Lonnie's greasy palm and rode my Harley-Davidson home humming "Pomp and Circumstance" into the wind. By the Pacoima exit I remembered that I had forgotten entirely to tell Alice about my conversation with Gridley.

Perhaps I did not choose my time well. Alice was standing on the toilet seat pouring water into the Creeping Charlie. Ellen, our youngest, was in the bathtub and she and I were making horns on her head out of bubble bath. Kip, his feet set precariously on the outskirts of adolescence, was shaving his imaginary beard over the sink.

"Alice," I said, "what would you think about moving?"

"Moving where?" she asked, holding the watering can aloft like a question mark.

"Well, I don't know," I said, shaping Ellen's bubble-horns into Brünnhilde braids and stepping back onto Kip's ankles.

"Almost cut myself," he complained in a tone not unlike his father's.

"Where?" asked Alice again. "You mean to a bigger house?"

"Well, maybe that too."

"I think we need to talk," she said, stepping down from the toilet lid. "Where's Topaz?"

"It's Wednesday. He's at ballet."

"Then we'll wait," she said.

* * * * *

Alice does not like to fight in front of the children. Personally I prefer it. Malthus and I never fought in front of the children; as a consequence the younger four persist in believing I left their father because he dropped the Beef Wellington on the floor one night.

Alice likes music when she fights, I like a fire. Alice likes to sit on the porch, I like to lie in bed. Alice says never fight where you make love. Everybody collects lore and fetishes through the years. I would like to endow a museum of lore and fetish.

We waited for Topaz. We first met Topaz years ago when he answered my ad for a live-in child care helper, but he has become friend, confidante, counselor, family. He's finishing up his M.A. in dance.

Finally he pulled into the driveway, turned his key in the lock, and stood before us in his mauve sweat suit, his lavender satin shoes slung over his shoulder. Topaz is six foot-three in his stocking feet, a fact which — together with his strong brow, iron jaw, and bronze visage — makes it highly unlikely anyone will ever venture a comment on his love of colorful garments.

"Ladies," he said, then leaned down to kiss us each.

"How was it?" I asked.

"Don't ask," he said, gripping his lower back. "I might be getting too old for this shit. Where're the kids?"

"In bed," said Alice.

"Asleep," I said.

"Not quite," she corrected.

"I see," said Topaz. "It's fight night."

"We just need to talk," said Alice. "On the porch."

"You two go right ahead," said Topaz. "Nana's back."

Alice put on a string quartet playing something resonant and mathematical, then cracked the window so we could hear faintly from the porch. The moon lit up the backyard like a crime light.

"Ah, that's better," said Alice, settling into her favorite wicker chair, the one with the high back that frames her head. The moon cast shadows under her cheekbones and silvered her hair, making her look regal though unaware of it, the way true royalty must be.

We sat in the quiet for a while. I could just make out a string of bunnies mashed up against the wire front of the barn watching us. Beneath their feet three hundred more went efficiently about the task of procreation.

"Hello, sweets," I called to them softly.

"I love you," Alice said to me, full face and direct in that way she had, looking at me with those gray eyes that were strong and soft at once. "Now what is this about moving?"

"I'm sorry," I said, because I was. "I should have told you sooner, but I let myself get distracted with the motorcycle."

"You tend to do that," she said in her non-judgmental, Margaret Mead voice.

"Gridley says I've got to get a job."

"What can she possibly have to do with our lives?"

"She calls them 'hostages to fortune,' " I said angrily.

"The children?"

I nodded. "She observes there are six of them."

"That's none of her business."

"She says I should finish up in the spring and get a job."

"Supposing you don't?"

"For starters she's the Chair of the Mabel Todd Huntington Fellowship Committee."

"Ah, the source of your Princely Sum. Why must everything always come down to money?"

"She's hinted before I might not be worthy of the Princely Sum. Remember the fellowship's subtitle."

"Yes. 'For Girls Who Support American Ideals.' "

"Exactly. The part about the ideals began to trouble her long ago, but now she's beginning to anguish over the girl part. I think she's noticed I'm a woman."

"God forbid," said Alice. "Do you think you could finish by spring, though?"

"I could finish by next Tuesday if I had to. I've just never had to before. I wanted to stay until I was properly educated."

"You do very well being improperly educated. In fact I think I prefer it." She looked through the pines at the moon; I looked across the yard at the bunnies. Three hundred of them. Something would have to be done.

"Any chance of finding a job around here?" Alice

asked, reaching out and slipping her fingers through mine.

"I'll try, of course. But it's not really very likely."

"We'll need to tell the children," she said. "And Topaz."

"Not to mention the rabbits," I said, pulling her chair close.

"So many hostages to fortune," she said, sheltering herself in my arms.

CHAPTER 3:
Appliances

The next day the toaster broke. Do you believe in metaphors? Let me explain a little about my personal cosmology.

In front of Malthus I always denied having a theory about anything at all, let alone the universe. I'm not sure why. It seemed to give me just the tiniest little edge over him. To others I let my philosophies leak out a little at a time according to their desserts, their attention spans, and my own mood at the moment.

But in a work of this sort I will hazard a broader treatment. Every event and every object in our lives stands for something larger but more elusive. Nothing is simply itself and nothing more. Look into your vegetable crisper, if you will, your sock drawer, your own dark pockets, and you will find clues that shimmer beneath the surface of the material world.

The problem with most of us is we have uncorrected vision problems. We may have glasses but we will not put them on. Perhaps we have dropped a contact lens somewhere on the deep-piled carpet of existence.

Which brings me to Henry James, who noticed that turn-of-the-century carpets had "figures" in them which if we would just open our eyes would become rewardingly apparent. Imagine, then, that life is a living-room carpet of good quality. The inattentive will walk on it for days and never notice it is Antron 500 in Sahara Gray, soil resistant, with a tight weave and double-jute backing. They never "experience" the carpet; they only pass over it like chewing camels. The trick is to get down on your hands and knees and crawl through it, preferably barefooted, to curl up in a ball and sleep on it, to wake up on it, to spill things on it, to remove yourself from it just a bit until the pattern comes slowly into focus.

This metaphor is beginning to bore me. Metaphors of vision have even been known to induce nausea. Let's try a nice detective metaphor. There is, let us say, a mystery at the heart of the fiction we are reading. The reader — as detective — goes in search of clues. How does she know what is a clue and what is a simple object or event, innocent of significance?

The master detective assumes initially there is *no such thing* as an innocent object or event. She stops along the way interrogating lamp-posts and dead cats, incidentally making herself ridiculous to passersby. But gradually, through great patience and a little luck, she amasses enough by way of object and event that when spread out all across her bed, or her breakfast table, or even her living room carpet they begin to group themselves into little piles of similarity. Aha, says the detective at the end of much rumination, and sends out little notes inviting the well-dressed suspects into the drawing room for a scene of revelation and finally accusation.

As Chief Inspector of my own little mystery I began to notice an odd pattern of breakdown, though I was volumes away from a solution. There was, as I have said, the little matter of the broken toaster. Next day I turned on my hair dryer and it sent out a puff of smoke and a lethal blast of asbestos. Then the refrigerator began to shudder whenever confronted with a tray of tap water. Next the hot-water heater died.

What message was existence tapping out to me over its ancient Morse code machine?

As I lay under the hot-water heater, pinned down by the amazing fact that both coils had gone out simultaneously, I realized I was losing this little war with termagant appliances. They — and not my six children — were becoming my hostages to fortune. I had a quick vision of the back yard glimmering in the sun, white with cast-off appliances that gleamed like elephant tusks.

I scrambled out from under the water heater and made for my writing room. From the topmost book shelf I carefully lifted down the little leather pouch that held my Aunt Vi's I-Ching coins. Crouching down on the braided rug, I gave them a toss across the hardwood floor. One almost rolled into the floor furnace. I leaned over the spread-out coins. "Fox who crosses great water gets tail wet," they said.

"I have always found betrayal the foulest of human impulses," I said one cool October evening, staring at the coffee pot's entrails laid out across the kitchen table.

"And so does most of the world," said Alice, wiping the last of the dinner plates.

"I find it particularly reprehensible."

"Especially in a coffee pot," she said, kissing the back of my neck.

"Especially in Malthus," I said, taking her damp hand in mine.

"Ah, in Malthus." She sat down across from me and picked up the Norelco thermostat, looking at it as if it were a strange shell washed up on the kitchen table. "There's really no accounting for Malthus."

"No," I said, "it would be futile to try."

"There is his childhood," she said with a twinkle.

"Yes, sweet," I said, turning the coffee pot on its side, "but we have all had unfortunate childhoods which in the telling one day begin to sound tedious and Byronic even to ourselves. Then we have the good grace to set aside our grievances and get on with it."

"Malthus' reminiscences do tend toward the operatic," she conceded.

"Thank you. I hate it when you're being fair."

"Not always," she said. "Sometimes you like it."

"Sometimes I like it very much," I said, accepting the thermostat from her outstretched hand and fitting it into place.

"But not with Malthusian topics."

"No," I said. "Inappropriate."

"Unnecessary."

"Superfluous."

"What's he done now?" Alice asked.

"He came over this afternoon."

"The very idea." Alice smiled.

"That's not all. He brought a girl. With curly hair the color of Mercurochrome."

"A girl?" said Alice. "Whatever for?"

"She was on his arm," I said, turning the tiny screw into the thermostat plate.

"A child?"

"She may have been twenty-four. Not fifteen minutes older."

"But Malthus is bald," she objected.

"Only in a wind. The wind wasn't blowing. He stipulates that they shall date only when the wind is not blowing. Besides, when you're twenty-four you don't notice details like that."

"I did, when I was twenty-four."

"He still looks a little like William Holden."

"She couldn't possibly know who William Holden is."

"Probably she's a film buff."

"With bad eyesight."

"And very bad taste," I said, giving the last screw a final turn and breaking off the head.

"What did he want?" asked Alice, reaching into a lower cabinet for the brandy.

I shook out the screw head and tossed it into the trash. Then I stood and slowly stretched myself, said "Shanti" three times with conviction, and ran cold water into the pot. "Want some coffee?"

"This," she said, lifting a tiny amber glass filled with brandy. "Want some?"

I shook my head. "I can't ask Lillian to make coffee if I don't mean to drink some."

"Lillian Coffee Maker?" said Topaz, sticking his head in the kitchen doorway. "Has Lillian survived surgery?"

"Too soon to tell," said Alice. "She's in guarded condition."

"Lillian's condition," I said, measuring in the Eight O'Clock, "was never very serious in the first place."

"Well," said Topaz, "give me a hit. I'm an optimist." He dragged a third chair in from the living room.

"You must be going out with Tom," I said, pushing Lillian's red start button and sitting down between Alice and Topaz.

He put his hand to his paisley tie. "How did you know?"

"That's easy," said Alice. "You don't usually wear

a tie, not to mention winter-white flannel trousers, and a double-breasted, burnt-sienna jacket."

"I like to think I'm always well-dressed and impeccably optimistic," said Topaz. There was silence. "Well, aren't I?"

"I wouldn't exactly call it optimistic," temporized my kind Alice.

"More like cynical," I said.

Topaz shook his head. "You ladies are harsh," he said. "Very harsh."

"But you are optimistic when you're going out with Tom," I said. "I wouldn't want you to be any more optimistic than that." I looked over at the coffee pot. Lillian was making soft, wheezing sounds.

"Too much optimism is bad for you," Topaz said, pouring himself some brandy. "Like for example anybody who thinks Lillian is actually going to make coffee is just too optimistic for this world."

"Of course she's making coffee," I said. "What else would she be doing?"

"Listen," said Topaz. We all looked at the coffee pot. "Listen to that Lillian. She sounds like she's dying. Just like the dryer. Lillian's got it too."

"There's nothing wrong with that dryer."

"It's old," said Topaz. "It's very, very old."

"Old is not dead," I said.

"In some cases," said Topaz. "In some cases old is dead. Ralph is very very old. Ralph scorched my white cords last night and seared the elastic in nine pairs of my designer jockey shorts."

"It's true dear," said Alice. "I hadn't wanted to mention it after the toaster and the hair dryer and the refrigerator. But Ralph burned up your red sweat suit this morning. I had to unplug him. He'd gone mad."

I put my head down on the table and banged it gently.

"But Lillian is fine," said Alice, as if in continuation.

"Lillian is not fine," I said from under crossed arms. "Lillian has consumption."

Topaz snorted. "Well, it can't get worse than this."

"But it *is* worse than this," I said lifting my head.

"Malthus came by today," explained Alice. "With a girl."

"We knew that," said Topaz. "We knew Malthus was straight. Didn't we know that?"

"She was no more than a child," I said.

"A young woman," Alice corrected.

"A very young woman," I said. "I believe she wore braces on her teeth."

Topaz poured himself another brandy, then he poured me one, then very gently he unplugged the feverishly huffing Lillian. "So what did the dude want?"

"My civil rights," I said. "He says if I get a job out of state I can't take the children or we'll be back at square one. He'll bring suit against me."

"He can't do that," Topaz said. "You got to work. Sad as it seems, everybody's got to work." He lifted the lid of the coffee pot and stared into steam.

Alice sat pale, knotting her hands. "He doesn't want the children, not really. He doesn't even like being with them. They're a chore to him."

"A duty," I amended. "A sacred duty."

"Asshole," said Topaz. "Keeps those kids whirling around on ferris wheels so he won't have to get real with them. Feeds them junk so they puke all night. Ask me, the man is an unfit parent."

"I just can't understand," said Alice, looking toward the ceiling as she does when she is afraid she will cry and thus spread her pain into the surrounding world, "I just can't divine what that man wants."

"That's easy," I said. "He wants fatherhood without the mess and obligation. He wants engraved cups, titles, admiration, and always, always to be right."

"Hell," said Topaz, "let's tell the dude he's right and split."

"Can you honestly fix your mouth to say, 'Malthus, you're right?' " I asked.

"No, I can't *honestly* do it, but I can do it quick enough. You learn that on the streets."

"Topaz, when have you ever been on the streets?" said Alice.

"We've all been on the streets," said Topaz. "You, me, Arden. It's Malthus walks only on wall-to-wall carpeting. The bottoms of his shoes look like glass. Give me the streets, I say, and my optimism."

"And Tom," I added.

"And Tom, of course," he agreed. "Now shape your mouths and say this with me: 'Malthus, honey, you eggzakly right.' "

* * * * *

26

That night I lay on my pillow listening to the electric blanket sending Morse code messages into the night. I raised up on my elbow. Alice, as well as her glowing control, slept peacefully. Her short gray hair had tufted up along the top of her head and her face was gentle as a child's. I would try to hold still and not wake her.

But Rosemary had definitely begun heating up. My side of the control was not just clicking: it was flashing. Earlier I had argued with Alice that it was too soon to get out the electric blanket, notwithstanding the fact that I had broken into my flannel-shirt supply three days earlier.

Actually, as Alice was quick to point out, I simply hate electric blankets. Ever noticed how your comfort is none of their concern? They are bent only on making those little clicking sounds that magnify as you enter a dream state, until the racket nearly deafens you and at the very least terrifies you into a night of eternal wakefulness.

And the heat from electric blankets is flat. Not like the round heat of a good quilt or a fluffy comforter. Comfort, after all, is the issue.

Alice, however, loves electric blankets. What is the point of cold feet? she always says.

My mother gave us this blanket a year ago Christmas. The manufacturer had promised that should anything go wrong with the blanket we had fifty-nine days to pack it up in its original box (where two litters of kittens has subsequently been born), and include the original sales slip (which my mother had carefully stored away in one of her thirty-three thousand unmarked manila envelopes), and mail it (insured and postpaid) to a small island off the coast of Hong Kong.

Instead I was going to simply cut off my half of this electric blanket with the pinking shears at first sign of daylight.

I unplugged my side of Rosemary and settled back into my pillow, letting one foot travel over to Alice in hopes that a little calm and comfort might reach me though this warm conduit. But I kept hearing Topaz saying, "Malthus, you're exactly right."

It was true that Malthus would prefer being right to having six children to bring up. But I thought there must be some other way — short of murder — to deal with Malthus. It was time to do the kind of thinking called "problem solving," but I was never any good at systems analysis where my own life was concerned. I could only solve other people's problems.

I needed a darker, less lucid approach to trouble. Something along the order of a visit from a shaman. I closed my eyes, withdrew my foot from Alice lest a brush with truth should inadvertently send her an electrical shock, and waited for the shaman to rest his hand on my shoulder.

At long last there was a clicking sound, not unlike Rosemary's earlier S O S, and a man dressed in black feathers and strings of red beads appeared beside me. His hair stood on end, and there were streaks of red over his brows and slashes of black across his glinting cheeks. The clicking was coming from a black painted gourd he kept whirling next to my ear. His breath smelled like dead chickens.

"They tell me from the beyond," he said, "that your dryer has seen God."

"Ralph and I have never been close," I said, "but I do know he caught fire day before yesterday."

"Just so," he said. "Your Ralph is no longer in need of repair."

"You might have come earlier."

"We never know," he said, casually flinging a string of beads over his shoulder, "either what to repair or when to repair it." His tone implied inefficiency was a virtue.

"You repairmen are all alike," I said. "I've heard this before."

"True repair begins in the heart of the broken," he said, "even before breakdown begins."

"That doesn't make any sense," I said.

"Your heart is like a clenched fist. I can't explain to a fist. You've got to open it first." Then he slid the handle of the gourd into my tight fingers, and with his hand on mine shook the gourd three times.

"Now put your foot on Alice," he advised, and was gone.

"What's the matter?" asked Alice, suddenly sitting up in bed. "Your foot's cold as ice."

"I can't sleep," I said. "I think Rosemary has crossed over."

Next morning the smog was strangely illuminated. The cool and subtle chill of fall had slipped back into Indian summer. The air smelled like hot tar. Topaz and I sat on the front porch drinking instant coffee. We liked to get up early so we could sit stunned for a while before the children woke.

"I hate instant coffee," said Topaz with satisfaction.

"You miss Lillian," I said.

"And I hate that garish sky." It was a tangerine color with streaks of gray. A little overdone, perhaps, but Topaz would have applauded it on any other morning, providing the coffee was decent.

"Red clouds at morning," I hazarded, then trailed off, not remembering if this condition boded good or ill.

"Shepherd lore," he said. "I hate shepherd lore and all that other honky pastoral horseshit."

We sat silent. I was pretending that the roar off the San Diego Freeway was really the tide coming in. "I had a dream," I said.

"And I hate listening to other people's dreams. Most of all, I hate that."

"What was it about?" asked Hillary from the front door.

"An Indian came and told me the dryer was dead. Now come and kiss me. I'm exhausted."

"Me too."

"Then why'd you get up so early?" said Topaz, reaching for the morning paper with his slippered foot.

"I have to be first whip today. Kip said so."

"What's Kip doing?" I asked.

"He's in your writing room typing. He's not supposed to be in your room, is he? What's he typing? He keeps saying, " 'Shit, shit, shit.' "

"The three hundred letters," I said. "You know, the job letters. I'm paying him twelve cents a letter."

"I don't want to move away," said Hillary, snuggling down between my feet like a terry cloth bunny. "I like it here. I don't want to live in a foreign country where the money is weird and nobody will understand my words."

"Where's my cornet?" asked Arthur, taking Hillary's place in the doorway. "I looked all over and I can't find it."

"It's not Tuesday," said Topaz, leafing past the news to find Ann Landers. "You don't need your cornet today."

"I need it. We're having an assembly, and I need my cornet.

"Ask Jamie."

"Jamie's sick."

"What's the matter with Jamie?" I asked

"She wants to see you," said Alice, handing Arthur his cornet over Hillary's head.

"Hillary," said Topaz, "if you're going to be first whip, you got to get Max and Ellen up and dressed. You got to have more system about you or this family is going to drop off into the vortex."

"What's a vortex?" asked Hillary.

"NOW!" roared Topaz, and the doorway closed.

We three adults sat and listened to the freeway tides. I had a powerful impulse to visit the Le Brea Tar Pits today. I didn't know if it was my dream or the whiff of tar in the smog this morning or my desire to cut my seminar in Colonial American Literature. A little Cotton Mather goes a very long way. I got up to see Jamie.

She was lying under two quilts and a heap of stuffed animals, her straight hair flamed out over the pillow and her face nowhere to be seen. I sat down on the edge of her bed and rubbed her back. Hillary read my uplifted eyebrow and led Ellen off to the living room with their clothes piled on one arm.

"What is it, Jamie?" I said.

She rolled over on her back and gave me an odd little smile. "I've started my period," she said softly.

Of course I had prepared her very carefully for this moment. But I had not known to prepare myself. I felt a little sob rising up from a deep place. I wanted to take my daughter's hand and lead her off to the women's hogan where we could laze around in good company, tossing sticks on the fire and telling each other complicated stories that seemed simple. Or simple stories that seemed complicated. "I love you," I said. "Can I get you anything?"

"No Mom," she said. "I took care of everything."

"You can stay home if you like."

"Are you going to school?"

"I thought I might take personal leave," I said. "I have a strange desire to go see the La Brea Tar Pits today."

"I think I'm about due for personal leave myself," she said, flinging back the quilts.

You can believe I bundled her up carefully in that sidecar. There we all were, revving our engines: Topaz in our old school bus with Kip, Hillary, Arthur, and Max; Alice in her Volvo with Ellen waving out the passenger window; and Jamie and I on the Harley — all going our different ways, together.

The sky was still streaked with orange like a

broken egg, and there was the smell of burnt toast in the air.

I had forgotten to eat anything. Today I would eat lunch with my daughter. We roared up the freeway ramp and I stole a sideways glance at her. She was wearing my Amelia Earhart white silk neck scarf and her blowing hair picked the orange right out of the sky.

CHAPTER 4:
Combination Plate

The La Brea Tar Pits freely translated means, "The the tar pits tar pits."

We hung over the guard rail staring into one of the prehistoric pools of thick bubbling tar that had once been Los Angeles. Bone-white bones were embedded all around the unmoving, petrified rim of the outer circle, while other bones floated inside the moiling inner circle of molten tar that was chuffing and working toward something, until the something pulled itself into a clear, quivering black bubble that held its tenuous shape against more chuffing and suddenly — pop — it gave in and joined the moving sludge once more.

What had drawn the giant owners of these bones — some soaring, some lumbering — toward their doom? Thirst? Not mere thirst, or hunger, I thought, dismissing the rumbling in my stomach. Not physical thirst and hunger, but the symbolic as well. They came, like Eve, seeking knowledge. Even as I, Arden Benbow, had come on the wingéd Harley with Jamie, the virgin daughter, both of us following the smell of tar to these pits, now.

But what was the message? I turned to the explanatory plaque on my left and tried to imagine the face of my shaman superimposed on it. I let my hands fall at my sides, open. "Ancestral bones," I said out loud.

"I beg your pardon," said an elderly gentleman standing next to me.

Jamie pretended she was reading the bronze plaque under a mastodon jawbone.

"Metamorphosis," I said under my breath.

"Lunch," said Jamie, pulling me toward the glaring parking lot.

"Jamie," I said, kick-starting the Harley, while she settled herself into the sidecar, "I'm sorry I embarrassed you. I'm a little preoccupied lately."

"You get worse when you don't eat," she said in a motherly tone.

"I had this dream last night . . ."

"Tell me on the way," she said, pointing up Wilshire Boulevard and the Olvera Street that waited inevitably beyond.

The smell of tar seemed to follow us. Air in greater Los Angeles was definitely becoming out of the question. I could remember in my own lifetime skies improbably blue, day after day. Now you could not see very far or breathe very well. Surely these things — sight, breath — were basic. Perhaps it was after all time to pack up the wagon train and head east. Perhaps Professor Gridley was a minor angel sent down from the goddess to startle me into making the right move. A very minor angel, but an angel nevertheless. And celestial news often was delivered by improbable messengers.

Like my shaman, disguised last night as the cosmic Maytag man making a house call. And what was it he had said? Repair begins in the heart of the broken? Even before breakdown begins? Their talk — like their costuming — was intended to throw you off, to leave you groping through strange metaphors that evaporated in the mind like cotton candy on the tongue, before you could apprehend them.

That was what happened if you approached metaphors in a head-on kind of way. Usually I simply pack more metaphors around the main one as if they were green tissue paper around a particular succulent avocado. "Hence, the tar pits," I said out loud.

Luckily Jamie had not heard me. She was looking up at the tall, glinting office buildings through whose shady corridor we traveled. Looking up always makes me feel a little imperious, but she seemed to be toying with the idea of feeling insignificant. I would buy her Mamacita's largest combination plate and stop plaguing her with my bones and my dreams.

We left the Harley at one of those parking lots

that charges $39.95 an hour, with an attendant who looked alarmingly like Lonnie, then dashed among the flying cars, risking death for some good Mexican food.

Mexican food calms the nerves, cures that state of mind my Aunt Vi called "the luna," and confirms you in any healthful resolutions you might have made in a moment of abandon.

Olvera Street, oldest street in Los Angeles! It begins at either end with a running fountain and a boys' marimba band. In between are carts filled with rubber lizards, huaraches, toy watches, sticky bright suckers, serapes, Mexican wedding shirts, leather whips, and paintings of John F. Kennedy on black velvet. Also there are tasteful shops selling fragrant hand-dipped candles and wonderful ceramics and silver jewelry too. But everything runs together — the crude and the refined, the gauche and the tasteful — into a blended kind of art that makes you laugh and cry at the same time, as if all the while that's what art was striving to be: a combination plate.

To find a really good Mexican restaurant you have to apply this principle: the best food is always accompanied by a lamentable decor. Red Naugahyde booths and chairs, red formica tables with chrome legs, beer posters on the wall showing human sacrifice (Quetzalquatl with a knife poised over a young woman in a state of disarray on a stormy night), and a jukebox streaked with floating colors and love laments.

Mamacita's place perhaps goes a step beyond most because of her fondness for plastic flowers which cascade down from fluorescent fixtures, hand rails, rafters, and the tables themselves.

Mamacita greeted us at the door, enfolding us in

deep and fragrant hugs. Said to be in her mid-eighties, she admits to sixty-five. Curiously doll-like in her dress of white dotted swiss, her sash and silk corsage of lilac, Mamacita lead us toward our table. We followed her uplifted plastic menus and the rhythmic tap tap of her white patent leather pumps.

"Jesus," said Mamacita sitting down with us, "my feet are killing me." Which one is this? she wanted to know, inclining her lacquered and faintly blue coif in Jamie's direction.

"You remember Jamie, second born, eldest daughter," I said. Jamie was studying, with great concentration and perhaps a little alarm, the flyblown virgin in the beer poster over Mamacita's shoulder.

"I knew your great-grandmother," said Mamacita to Jamie, sighing as she slipped her feet out of her shiny pumps. "She was a wonderful woman. Rode around on the red car, you know, the electric car, giving things. Two brown shopping bags. Taking things to people who didn't have nothing. Clothes, I'm talking about. Food. You never knew this by her. She didn't say."

With a little flourish, Mamacita handed us each a plastic menu. "Arden," she said, "remember that teacher friend of yours? The one who graded everything on the plate. 'A-minus for the chicken taco,' she'd say. 'B-plus for the chili relleno.' "

"She was a tough grader," I said. "Actually she didn't believe an A could exist on earth. Only in heaven was there a pure A chili relleno."

"Well I'm telling you today we got an A-plus chili relleno on the number four combination plate, made by Maria herself." Mamacita struggled momentarily under the table with her shoes, then rose and enfolded a startled Jamie in her arms. "Your great-grandmother was a wonderful woman," she said. "You got her eyes." And she disappeared into the kitchen.

"Do you think that's true," Jamie said, "that I look like her?"

"Don't you remember her?" I asked.

"I remember all those bracelets on her arms and the sound they made clacking against each other whenever she raised her hands. And I remember her rings, one on every finger. And I remember that baby picture we have of me sitting in the sunlight on a white blanket and she's sitting in a wicker chair behind the potted lemon tree — you can hardly see her in the shadow — knitting something. She seems not to be looking at me, but she seems to know I am there." Jamie rolled her flimsy restaurant fork up tight in a paper napkin. "Almost as if she makes it possible for me to be there."

"Exactly," I said, staring down into the steaming map of Mamacita's number four combination plate.

CHAPTER 5:
Dropping By

And who else made existence possible? My Uncle Ukie, that's who. Uke the Duke. Half shaman himself, he might know what this dream of mine meant. Ancestral bones. Yes. He would know the meaning of this dream.

Jamie and I picked up the Ventura Freeway and made for Toonerville, clover-leafing along from there until we hit Los Feliz Boulevard. Was the goddess going to require I relinquish by semester's end my freeway systems, perhaps even my Harley-Davidson 500?

We rode through shade now, bumping along the crumpled-up concrete streets, drizzled with dried tar, streets disheveled by giant tree roots and civic neglect. I could not resist a quick turn down my grandmother's street. In front of her green frame house I turned off the engine. Her ancient jacaranda laced us with shade. Slowly we eased off our helmets and breathed in the silence and the spirit of my grandmother.

I saw myself, my child self here, the one playing in the dirt with her cousins at the side of the house next to the sleeping porch where my mother had slept as a girl — tucked into cots and double beds with her six sisters — or hanging around in the kitchen listening to great aunts speaking Spanish so fast it sang around my head like a thousand swooping birds, while they patted thin the flour tortillas as big as my head, or rolled up masa inside corn husks, tied them with string and set the rellenos into the white enamel steamer for Sunday dinner, while my uncles, standing at the sink, tossed back shots of whiskey or tequila out of jelly jars. My aunts talked about their girlhoods at Lake Elizabeth, lisping the z sound out so softly — Elithabeth — you could almost see bright waves lapping the shore, while the undercurrent of uncle tones pronounced repeatedly that this or that was just a piece of *cangada,* that the past was a dead thing. Never look back, they said. Meanwhile my cousin Della and I would sneak behind the house to the dark bunk house where as boys these same uncles had slept in bunk beds that seemed to rise several stories. We would breathe in the old fox smell and run laughing out into the sunshine, where my Aunt Thelma would be talking to her chickens, then round the wood hen house where we would look for messages chalked there by tramps saying these people will feed you and turn you loose.

"Look," said Jamie, reaching up from the sidecar to touch my shoulder. "Her garden." The garden had gone to sticks and thin dirt. Tomato stakes stood lifeless, while up close to the house the shrubs grew rank and devouring. The earthen pots she had painted herself in bold reds, blues, greens, yellows were tumbled and chipped, their marbles (these she said made the plants grow better; always use marbles, nails for iron, a windmill if you have one) scattered and strewn in time like her own thirteen children.

Never look back, Ukie would say, hooking his thumbs into his silver belt and letting lazy eyelids fall over deep brown eyes. The family philosophy. For six generations they had wandered through Southern California on their Spanish land grant — her people — moving on when cattle died, when floods came, when someone fell in love or died or gave birth or grew restless, never recording, never claiming, until finally they had finished here in this small house, unsure even to whom it now belonged.

We put our helmets on. I eased out the clutch and we rolled forward.

There was an ominous red sports car parked in the driveway behind my uncle's pick-up. "It's Daddy's," Jamie confirmed, standing up in the side car and slipping off my jacket and the spare helmet. "Kip said not to tell you, it would only make you mad."

"It does make me mad," I said, "but it's not his business to edit reality for me. His father used to do that and look where it got him."

I had gone too far. Sometimes I forget that the kids are related to their father. Sometimes Malthus forgets it too, witness the tarty red car with only two seats into which Jamie and I now stared. She reached in and ran her hand over the black leather passenger seat.

"Daddy's still got the sedan," she said, reading my mind but staring into the seat. "He kept it for us kids."

"I'm sorry," I said. "You have his genes and I love you. I love *all* your genes now and forever in whatever combination and recombination."

"We should have told you."

"You were afraid of my wrath, poor children, and rightly so," I said, tucking my arm in hers and leading her toward the door. "Tired, love?"

She was shaking her head no, when Uncle Ukie opened the door and clasped us both to the giant blue and purple morning glories embroidered across the chest of his favorite cowboy shirt. "Christ," he said, releasing us at last, "how the hell are you? Rosie'll be sorry as hell she missed this."

Rosie was a salad chef at Walt Disney and worked days, while Ukie built space ejection seats for Lockheed on the night shift. It was a marriage made in heaven.

Across the room, seated on a plaid early-American

43

couch, his arm protectively resting over but not touching the tender shoulders of his Intended, lurked Malthus. Under the best circumstances Malthus looks a little avuncular; today he looked like a well-dressed and well-fed vampire.

Alice says I am neither accurate nor fair whenever I have to describe Malthus to people who've never seen him. She says he is quite attractive and bears a subtle resemblance to William Holden. I maintain that vampires in movies do tend to be attractive, having a certain *je ne sais quoi.* Therefore I am not demeaning Malthus. Not exactly.

At any rate, we all nodded amiably and affirmed that yes we had all met. Ordinarily Malthus would have risen at the arrival of what he liked to call "a lady," but either he believed that I no longer qualified for that appellation or that in the home of my colorful though barbaric relatives, politeness might be in bad taste.

Malthus viewed my family as a collection of crudely-wrought but amusing bric-a-brac that somehow had acquired value through time, like Fiestaware. As if to prove the point, a naked baby ran past the sliding glass door. Malthus stared.

"That's Dawn," explained my uncle. "Star's in the bedroom stringing her bow. Moonlight left them here while she job hunts."

Uncle Ukie had named all his unborn daughters and granddaughters one night while lying in a foxhole in Argonne during World War II.

Star streaked down the hall in a pair of pink Lollipop underpants, a bow slung over her naked shoulder and several arrows clutched in her left hand, careened through the front door, and slammed it behind her.

"Ready," screamed Star's small voice from beyond the front door.

Ukie casually strolled to the patio door and opened it wide, picked up the wet Dawn, who had evidently been circling a rainbird, stashed her under his arm, strolled back across the living room, opened the front door wide, then said in a calm voice, "Now nobody move."

There was a whizzing sound and a thunk as an arrow flew through the open front door, past our unbelieving eyes in the living room, and lodged itself outside in a bale of hay with a bull's-eye fastened to it.

"Not quite, honey," said my uncle to the invisible Star. "Aim her up and left."

Another whiz-thunk. I leaned my head cautiously. On target.

Malthus rose, keeping the backs of his knees pressed tight against the couch, and cleared his throat.

"That's right, sport," said my Uncle Ukie. "You wanted to talk to me about something. Just one more!" he called to the archer on the front porch. Malthus sat down quickly and well back in his seat.

There was another whiz, after which my small but triumphant cousin burst in smiling, her bow slung across her bare chest.

Ukie tousled Star's dark curls and returned the naked Dawn to her rainbird. "Why don't we go into the kitchen?" he said to Malthus. "And Arden, honey, you could take Star into the garage to check on her turtle."

"Her turtle?" I asked.

My uncle, though he does not wear spurs, manages to jingle when he walks. He flashed me a wink and jingled off to the kitchen, followed by Malthus and the family's three-legged dog.

I looked at Monica. Her pensive eyes were fixed on the pensive portrait of my uncle over the mantle. It's a charcoal drawing called "The Old Fisherman," mass-produced in Guaymas and sold to tourists for $49.95 American. Years ago on the Fourth of July a photo-journalist had taken his picture on the fishing pier, from which an enterprising youth had made the prototype.

Though my uncle is neither old nor a fisherman, the sketch captures a certain reality. Something, I think, about the eyes, about the way their sense of amusement balances out the pain in the face. The same people who haunt the world's gift shops searching for Don Quijotes in wood, in shellacked burlap, lacquered bread dough, oils, brass, clay, wire, pewter, always stopped before the old fisherman, as Monica now did.

"So what's the deal with the turtle?" I asked gently, startling both Monica and Jamie.

"It's dead," said Monica.

"It's taking a nap," said Star, putting her hand in mine and opening the hall door into the smell of afternoon garage.

My uncle's garage, I knew, was filled with hats and kites hanging in rows from the ceiling, suspended by fishing leader. The dead turtle would seem a little incidental in an atmosphere like that. I edged through the clutter in the darkness and swung open the big door, letting in air and light.

"Where is it?" said Jamie from the back. Monica was standing with her head tilted back staring at all those hats and the suspended kites with eyes stenciled on them.

"Here he is," said Star, squatting down next to a dime-store turtle spread-eagled between a rusty set of golf clubs and a stuffed elk. "Grandpa made these marks so when Jennifer moved we would know she was really alive."

Around each outstretched turtle foot a crescent had been drawn in pencil on the concrete.

"I had a turtle once," Monica said in a strange, faraway tone. A slight breeze stirred through the kites and hats.

Star lay thoughtfully down next to her turtle and stared into its sunken eyes.

"We're probably getting married, Malthus and I," Monica said, as if to the dead turtle.

Those of us who had been breathing stopped.

From behind us came a faint jingle and a whiff of Aramis. Uncle Ukie, his arm around Malthus' shoulder, solemnly pronounced, "Never look back."

"Beats the hell out of me," said Uke the Duke, later, resting his crossed cowboy boots gently on the coffee table and flipping off the cap of my beer bottle. The happy couple had driven off in their vile red sports car, and Jamie — having curled up companionably with her two young cousins — had

47

drifted off to sleep. "The only wedding I honest-to-Jesus enjoyed was when you and Alice got hitched in your back yard. But a church wedding. And me best man in a tuxedo. That ain't really my style. Malthus, he had me saying yes before I knew what hit me."

"Monica would probably know what you mean."

"And that's another thing. I like Monica."

"I do too."

"It was different when Malthus married Frances. Frances could take care of herself."

"She was a grownup, all right. Every time Malthus was wrong and she was right, she wrote it down in a little book. With dates and everything. As evidence. The kids say when she started volume two he asked for a divorce."

"Monica's a world away from Frances," said Ukie solemnly. "She wouldn't know to write things down." Then brightening a little he said, "She liked that kite I gave her. You think so? And the special string?"

Ukie's special string had been developed at Lockheed for use in outer space. He liked it because it did not break. Though he did, on occasion, cut it. I remember one Sunday afternoon he came out to the valley to visit Alice and me. He and I were in the yard, leaning against the back fence, watching his blue kite ducking and darting so far away that the string in his hand barely moved. Under our feet three hundred bunnies turned softly in their sleep. I heard the kitchen door bang shut — as if from far away — and saw Alice starting across the yard to call us to dinner. I put my hand on his arm and nodded toward Alice. All this we did quietly, as if we — along with the kite — were nodding in space. He took his big pearl-handled knife out of his pocket, opened it up, and drew the blade silently across his space string.

"Yes," I said, "she really liked that kite."

CHAPTER 6:
The Tower

Whenever I stand nose to nose with my mother I am obliged to acknowledge kinship. My mother calls these noses "aquiline." One more degree either in size or curve and they would look broken.

I now guide my own nose carefully past my mother's and kiss her cheek. She smells of powder base and My Sin.

When I was a kid, the woman across the street, whose house was hidden behind a jungle of untamed shrubberies, would come out from time to time and yell at my mother. She always yelled the same thing and never itemized her complaint. "Miss Hollywood!" she would scream, and then disappear into the shrubs. This was after my father died and my mother discovered cosmetics, along with the fact that, although nature isn't always right, Clairol is.

My father had liked her nose, and her long dark hair that fell far below her waist, and her big family. He liked to sit in her mother's kitchen and practice his Spanish.

To be perfectly honest my mother did not want to sit in her mother's kitchen and practice her Spanish. Having been raised with twelve brothers and sisters whose clothes were cut all from the same bolt of cloth — at least they're clean, my grandmother would tell them — my mother was more than ready to try something else.

Not that she didn't love her mother. She adored her mother. They all did. And they all sat around her bedside when the virgin appeared to her, beckoning. And they all grieved and cried and moved apart from each other in their grieving.

But as a young woman my mother was simply not willing to sit in her mother's kitchen and learn Spanish after having assiduously not learned it for twenty-five years.

"We are not Mexicans," she would say. "We are not Indians. We are Early Californians."

I hold her now and kiss her big nose.

She pushes me away laughing. "Let's have coffee," she says, leading me into the kitchen. "How's Alice? How're the kids?"

"Fine," I say. "Everybody's fine. The kids are

risking life and limb on Thunder Mountain with their father: Alice is home waiting for the plumber. She sends her love." I move the Sunday paper off a chair and sit down. "Where's Shelden?" I ask dutifully, Shelden being the successful man my mother stands behind. My mother says behind every successful man there's a successful woman.

She nods toward the kitchen floor. "Where else?"

She means he is in his office two floors below, even though it is Sunday, and that compulsion is an endearing quality when it generates money. Their apartment, curiously placed on top of these offices, can only be reached by an outside staircase leading up to their terrace. All of this is on a busy street in Glendale, so that the terrace is enveloped — except after hours — in smog and deafening traffic sounds.

Strangely enough both my mother's husbands sought, each in his turn, to place my mother in high, inaccessible places, my father having selected the topmost pinnacle of a hill in Silver Lake for our home and my stepfather this moated castle. My mother has always interpreted their desire to isolate her as a compliment.

"So," she says, placing a filled cup before me, "you want a reading." She opens a kitchen drawer, the kind filled with Green Stamps and string, and takes out her Tarot cards, wrapped in a green silk scarf that must say Vera in one corner. She removes the scarf and hands me the deck. "Here," she says, "put these in your bra."

I look at her. "OK," she says, "then stick them in your pants. Over your stomach. That's second best." She sits down with her coffee. "Now think about the question."

"The question, the question," I repeat. "Did I ever tell you what Gertrude Stein said on her deathbed?"

"*Your* question, not Gertrude Stern's question," and she fixes me with her dark eyes that say, "I've got your number."

"The question is —" I begin.

My mother holds up her hand like a crossing guard. "Don't tell. Don't tell me the question. Just think it. Haven't I ever given you a reading before?"

"Aunt Vi did, that summer in Mexico. She called me the Queen of Cups."

"Vi," she says, her eyes misting with thoughts of her dead sister.

I put my hand on hers. "Queen of Cups," I repeat.

"Good," says my mother, setting the memory of her sister aside for later. "We'll use the queen for your significator card. Shuffle."

"Any special way?"

"Whatever comes to you."

I retrieve them from my stomach, shuffle, hand them to my mother. Her long silver fingernails curve around the pack. She riffles through, quickly spots the Queen of Cups, and places her face-up on the glass table.

"Now cut the cards into three piles. Use your left hand."

I do as she says and watch her pick up the three piles with her left hand, beginning with the first I set down. Now she deals, putting a card exactly over my Queen of Cups, then one on top of that but crosswise. These she uses as the center of a cross, then runs four cards up one side. I try not to notice

53

what's on the cards but only watch them in an unfocused way, as if they are goldfish floating on the aquarium-like surface of the glass table.

She sits back to consider. I watch her face. Notice her new sun blotches beneath her make-up, the delicate pink skin beneath her short, bleached hair, the soft blue folds of skin on her eyelids.

I am determined not to panic when I see the Death card, for see it I will. Slowly I focus my eyes; the goldfish become bright cards. There it is in the lower right-hand corner — Death — but mitigated by a fair number of naked people laid out here and there with pleasant expressions on their faces.

I get up to pour us some more coffee.

"I'm not going to lie to you, Arden," says my mother. "You're an adult."

"More or less," I say. "Just read the cards. Pretend you're at a fund-raiser for the Fatimas of the Fez and you're reading cards to make money for the Shriners' Hospital. You don't know me from Adam. I'm just another Fatima."

"In that case," says my mother, her forehead falling back into lines of general, lifelong pleasantness, "you got a hell of a card covering you."

"Covering me?"

"See your significator, the Queen of Cups?"

"No," I say. "I can't see the queen. There's a card on top of her with lightning bolts coming out of it."

"Exactly," she says, lifting the crosswise card so I can see the lightning bolts better. "The Tower."

The Tower has flames bursting out of its windows where the lightning has struck and there are two people falling head-first out of an upper story. In the upper-left corner a solitary crown drifts skyward, licked by flames. This does not bode well. I lift my eyebrows in inquiry.

"Too materialistic," says my mother, tapping her long silver fingernail on the glass next to the card. "That's what the crown means. They know why they're getting evicted but they didn't know in time."

"Am I materialistic?" I say, a little ruffled.

"No," she says, "you're too absent-minded. In fact you might not be those people at all. The card might just mean sudden change, new ways of thinking. That's your atmosphere card. Things must be changing at home."

In my mind I convert the falling people into a plummeting dryer and air conditioner and the card makes perfect sense.

"Now this card," says my mother, putting the crosswise card back down on the Tower, "this is your Hanged-Man card. That's a very good card to have. It means you've gotten just so far and thought that was enough. But it's not. You've got more to learn. See the rays of light coming out of his head. He's a special person. He'll learn, all right, but not unless he gives in first. See how he just hangs there upside-down without complaining. That's how you learn something."

"Hanging upside-down?"

"Why not?" she says. "Stranger things have happened. Now this card down here —"

"It's upside-down," I interrupt.

"I can see that," she says, and waits.

"Sorry," I say.

"This is behind you. You had it, but you can't have it anymore. That's the four of Wands. Reversed."

There are two people again, but this time they wear garlands on their heads and they stand in front of a castle that is not on fire.

"Rest after labor," says my mother, "peace and prosperity. Too bad it's passing away."

"But it's upside-down. Maybe that means it's not passing away."

"No, it means it was never as good as you thought it was, but it was good. Just not that good. See?"

I nod.

"Now this lady here, the nine of Pentacles, she's a lucky lady. Too bad that's the past."

"The past again?"

"The recent past. Pentacles in general mean money. Nine means completion. Too bad." She shakes her head.

"What about the future?" I ask.

"I'm coming to that. Ah, the Lovers. You got a lot of major arcana here."

"Who's that between the Lovers?" I ask, fearing the worst.

"That's Cupid, of course."

"His hair looks a little fiery," I say.

"Well, you can read this card as temptation. Or you can say it's about the brain and your feelings, that they get along together. Which I think they do." She smiles.

"I'm just a Fatima," I remind her.

"Whatever. But this is the card that crowns you. The next card is what's before you. This is your near future."

She taps her fingernail beside a card where two people sit in a boat being poled across a river. Nobody faces forward, and there are six tall swords sticking straight into the bottom of the boat. It is pretty clear they'll never make it.

"Six of Swords. Six is a very positive number, but swords tend to be about bad times. Let's say the six kind of makes the scene the slightest little bit more optimistic. Basically the card means you're going on a journey. Here it hooks up with the Hanged-Man card. You're going to travel and gain wisdom. But you can't be pushy about it. Sometimes you are just the least bit pushy."

"There are swords stuck into that boat," I observe.

"You can't have everything," she warns. "And besides, the Death card does not mean death. It means change." Her finger moves on to the fated card. "It comes at the bottom of the staff. What the querent fears. The querent seems to fear change." She looks at me, lifting a slim black eyebrow into the shape of a question mark.

I look carefully at the card. Death wears black armor and rides a white horse with red eyes. Under the horse's feet various people have been trampled to death. Of course I fear change.

"The next card shows family opinion."

More swords. The seven of Swords. A sneaky-looking man in a red hat has picked up five of the swords and is making off with them Two other swords stick in the ground. Like the swords sticking out of the boat, these bode ill for the querent.

"Seven is a good number," says my mother. "It means inner work. You got a lot of that to do. The cards keep saying so. The divinatory meaning is A Plan That May Fail. The family's opinion is that your plan is no good."

"I never had a plan in my life," I protest.

"The only other thing the card can mean is somebody is stealing something."

"Ah ha," I say. "Malthus. He's trying to take the children away."

"Again?"

"He says he will if I try to take them out of state."

"Then find a job in California. It's your home, after all. It's your children's home. What does Alice think of traipsing half way across the country at her age? And Topaz? You'll never find another baby-sitter like Topaz."

"The querent's family does not fear change to the degree the querent herself does. And I would stay, if I could, and will if I can. But colleges and universities don't like to hire somebody who's been trained in their state. They think it makes for weakened stock."

"Like the Roosevelts," says my mother dreamily, "and their crooked teeth." Briefly she contemplates this dental tragedy, then leans over the spread of cards once more. "Let's finish the reading."

"I love you very much," I say. "Thank you for reading my cards."

"There's two more," she reminds me. "The Magician. You'll like that card. This is what you hope."

An androgynous person in a red cape stands before a table with objects spread out on it that look rather like the weapons in a Clue game. There are red and white flowers blooming all around the Magician's head and feet. Her left hand points toward the flowers and her right holds aloft an object that looks like a runner's baton.

"See his outfit!" exclaims my mother, brightening over the possibility of fashion. "That beautiful crimson cloak, and underneath, the white tunic falling softly about his waist."

"And the sweet scalloped neckline," I add.

"Yes . . . red is for passion, white is for purity. The magician draws strength form the earth and changes it into divine energy. See that wand?" she says, tapping her silver nail on the runner's baton. "That's your talent, your poetry."

"What's that clutter on the table?"

"All the suits," she says. "Pentacles, swords, cups . . . you name it. He works with all of those, holding together the material and the spiritual world."

"Hocus-pocus, hocus-pocus dominocus," comes my stepfather's voice through the opening terrace door. Then his hand comes through, fingers twirling spasmodically; next he prances bent-kneed across the living room and into the kitchen.

My mother scoops the cards together and quickly wraps them in her green scarf. Then she turns her cheek up for his kiss. He obliges her, then disobliges me with a matching kiss. "Are my girls having themselves a seance?" he asks, smoothly taking my mother's seat as she rises to prepare his lunch.

Shelden has been my stepfather longer than my father was my father, but he will never earn tenure with me. Years in rank do not count.

My mother throws a frozen steak patty into a ticking fry pan and steps back from steam and hot grease. "Honey, you remember Arden's about to graduate."

"Remember," snorts Shelden, "she's been about to graduate twelve years that I know of." He picks up my limp hand and gives it a just-kidding squeeze.

"I've really got to go," I say.

"Well give those wonderful kids our love," says my wonderful stepfather.

"Just a minute," says my mother, laying the bleeding steak patty gently on its bed of lettuce, covering it with toast, and neatly slicing through the nine millionth sandwich of her life. "I'll walk you out."

We stand close together on the terrace, all but engulfed by the din of horn and engine and stench, she leaning close and fragrant, saying into my ear, "The last card."

"The last card?"

"Your reading. We never finished. The last card is the World." She steps back and her eyes widen to accommodate the vastness of her vision. "That's your final outcome card. Androgyny, cosmic consciousness, the path of liberation. The Hanged Man, remember? Now he's upright and turned into a Naked Lady."

"I like that," I admit, guiding my nose around hers and holding her tight. "I like that very much."

"But you gotta work," she warns, letting me go. "I'm not going to lie to you."

CHAPTER 7:
Thanksgiving

"Alice is in the bathtub reading Trollope," I said. "Don't bother her, Arthur, ask me." Arthur is nine and very attached to Alice for all the right reasons, including the fact that they both play the cornet.

"Well," said Arthur, "I want to put those baby marshmallows into the jello and Hil says marshmallows in jello is tacky."

"Who's assigned jello?" I asked.

"Me."

"Then you decide, Arthur. You're the jello-master and you say."

We collided in a hug and he ran off to the kitchen.

"Thanks, dear," called Alice from the bathtub. "I need to collect myself a bit before the guests arrive. Come in, if you like."

There is something about a woman in a bathtub. What artist was it that painted hundreds and hundreds of women in bathtubs? Not all at once. I mean every day he got up, washed, breakfasted, and began painting a new woman in a new bathtub. A good way to spend a life, I thought, sitting down on the toilet lid. But what is it about women in bathtubs?

"When I'm in a bathtub," said Alice, as if in reply, "I feel like a mermaid, like I'm rejoining a world I spend the day cut off from." Gently she closed her novel and placed it on the breadboard that served as her reading desk whenever she read in the bathtub and then sank beneath the waters until she stretched out full-length underwater. I held my breath.

At last she sounded, nearly upsetting the breadboard and Trollope. "Remember, dear," she mused, redirecting rivulets of water around her eyes and plastering her hair back off her forehead, "the time you had been reading Sylvia Plath in the bathtub and when you went to teach "The Three Muses" the next day every page in your book fell out?"

"Actually they sort of shot up in the air and then floated down over the class. I brought them art that day, a fountain of art."

"As I recall you were embarrassed."

"That too. Art and embarrassment. Sounds like the title of a coffee table book, *Art and Embarrassment,* by Arden Benbow."

"According to the youthful Benbow," intoned Alice, holding out the sponge to me, "without embarrassment there can be no art."

"And without a beautiful woman," I said, running the sponge in circles over her back, "there can be no bathtub."

"Mommie," called a small voice from the hallway.

Sometimes I find I have momentarily lost sight of the fact that life is a series of interruptions. Alice pulled the plug.

"Yes Ellen," I called, "I'm coming."

She was standing in the doorway of the bedroom, with a huge checked apron wrapped around her waist, counting on her fingers. At the age of four she had become preoccupied with numbers. "How many?" she said, holding up two dimpled hands.

"How many what, duck?"

"People. For Thanksgiven."

"Thirteen," I said.

"Unlucky," said Topaz, walking by and threading a tie behind his collar, then sliding it rapidly back and forth the way people do just before they approach the tying of the knot.

"No," said Ellen. "Lucky."

"Why lucky?" said Topaz, stopping his tie-dance.

"Because I'm four and a half. And because I'm the napkin girl."

"Out of the mouths of babes." Topaz stooped down and kissed her, then looked up at me. "This is a lucky day."

"Because Tom's coming?" I guessed.

"Because Tom's coming and, as you and Alice have observed on more than one occasion, optimism always precedes his arrival." Here he did a little soft-shoe and came to rest with his right heel and right index finger pointing to a spot on the floor. Ellen leaned forward to see the object of his attention, then gave a little shrug.

"But," Topaz went on, resuming his usual proud posture, then crumpling down into false humility and genuine cunning, "dat ain' de haf of hit. Nawsa. Us darkies got a plan gwan bring trouble down on de big house."

"What big house?" said Ellen. "This one?"

"Command Module needs a meeting," said Topaz. "All kids in the kitchen double-quick and start cooking your little hearts out. You got your assignments. It's eleven-fifteen now and dinner's at oh-one-hundred."

The napkin girl ran off to the kitchen.

"I wish we had a room for meetings," Topaz said wistfully. "Right now we need a war room. We need flip charts, maps with little stick pins in them, plastic submarines . . ."

"You can come in here," said Alice, cracking the bedroom door. "I'm decent." She was wearing her blue dress with the large red poppies and looked a little like Alice B. Toklas, though it would not do to mention this resemblance to my love, who has never been much amused with that literary couple.

"Decent now and always," said Topaz, kissing her cheek and passing inside. "How's the buzzard?"

"Cooking," said Alice, clearing her pajamas and a box of animal crackers off our bed. "Champagne and real butter. I put it in three hours ago. Why do we need a meeting?"

"Strategy," he said, sitting down on the foot of the bed and fussing briefly over his trouser creases. "Now as I see it we got a two-pronged attack. First, we keep Malthus off-balance by telling the son of a bitch he's right all the time and plying him with liquor. Get him ready for the bargaining table with Arden later."

"What's the other prong?" I asked. "Isn't one prong enough?"

"Other prong's got to do with the Intended," said Topaz.

"What's the Intended?" asked Alice.

"Who, not what," corrected Topaz. "Malthus' Intended."

"Monica's not so bad," I said. "Let's leave her out of this."

"But she's crucial," objected Topaz.

"Why?" asked Alice. "She's not threatening to take the children. Malthus is."

"All I'm saying is this. Just let her get some kind of realistic idea what she's signing on for. That's all. Just don't protect her. Let life happen."

"You mean treat her like family, not like a guest?" Alice said. "Well why didn't you just say so?"

Topaz fell over backwards onto the bed.

"The field marshal's suffering a quinsy," I said, "a two-pronged quinsy, and shall be put to bed straight-away."

When the phone rang, Topaz was beating me over the head with a pillow. "It's for Ruth," yelled Max from the kitchen.

"Does a Ruth live here?" asked Topaz, pillow poised.

"Probably it's Ruth who is calling," said my Alice.

"Who's Ruth?" he and I said together.

"The orphan I was telling you about," said Alice in a whisper, as if Ruth were lurking under the dust ruffle. *You* remember."

"This is a confusing household," said Topaz. "I don't remember any orphan. Do I? Which orphan?"

"Arden, surely you recall. Explain again to Topaz. I'll take it in the kitchen."

"Well?" Topaz said after she'd gone.

"Orphan, orphan, orphan," I murmured, resolving in future to listen more carefully to my love. "Yes!" I said. "I've got it. Ruth Orphan. Her new executive assistant. You remember. Doesn't know how to dress?"

"Could be inconvenient," Topaz said judiciously.

"I mean a possible beehive. Alice is going to take Ruth under her wing, you know, network with her."

"And this poor unfortunate is coming here to learn taste and manners. She has my sympathy."

"Do you think," I said, running my eyes over my jodhpurs and red high-top tennis shoes, "I am not quite setting the proper example?"

Topaz whooped and fell back on the bed laughing.

Ruth came early. Dressed in a navy blue suit with red anchors on the sleeves. She wore red glasses that looked like they might be attached to her nose. The kind of glasses that made you think that halfway through dinner somebody would get up and take them gently off her nose and exclaim, "Why you're beautiful!"

Alice immediately bustled her off to the kitchen to solicit her help with some imaginary problem involving the turkey. Now Alice practically invented turkeys and I could tell this was a ruse to make the orphan feel needed.

I do believe in kindness but I do not believe in deceptions unless they are absolutely necessary. Have you ever studied a spoon in a glass of water? Face it, the senses are a real crap-shoot where reality is concerned. So why get up illusions for other people, particularly the maimed? I like to garnish kindness with a twist of irony.

Alice believes otherwise. So she kept opening the oven door, setting the bird on the counter, and getting Ruth to prick and wiggle wings and drumsticks experimentally.

You can't cook turkey like that. But Alice was in charge of turkey and I was in charge of enchiladas. To stay out of their way, I put my big orange crock on the dining room table and did all my cheese grating, olive chopping, and green onion dicing out there, while Jamie, my assistant, would nip into the kitchen to fry up hamburger and onions, or gather up spices, or search out tortillas from the refrigerator. I built up layers of enchiladas in the crock like they were archaeological levels in an ancient dig, the way my grandmother used to do.

"Homestyle," my grandmother called these great crocks of enchiladas. I watched my daughter scatter the last layer of grated cheese across the top of our family history.

Actually I smelled the Aramis before I sensed his ominous presence. Malthus was standing behind me and the enchiladas, Monica's forearm, wrist, and five fingers tucked under his arm for safekeeping. He was looking amused.

"Arden always makes enchiladas along with the turkey. Though actually the fact that Indians first introduced turkey to their conquerors ought perhaps to be sufficient acknowledgment of your ancestry."

I coiled myself.

Smoothly Topaz interposed himself between us. "That's right, Malthus. You're exactly right. Matter of fact I was just looking for you to give me some advice here about the wine." With one finger he guided Malthus toward the kitchen as if he were an expensive piece of furniture on wheels.

"It looks good," the Intended murmured behind me. "What is it?"

"My family," I said absently. "I mean, my family always had enchiladas because we're Chicanos on my mother's side. I didn't realize until I married that other people didn't eat them too. Malthus disabused me. Other people's delusions drive him wild," I said with satisfaction.

"Can I help?" she asked.

"No, I'm used to it."

"I mean with the dinner," she said, sliding her shoulder bag along her recently liberated arm and onto a dining room chair.

"My part's finished," I said, sliding myself into the neighboring chair and patting the third in invitation. "Sit. I haven't seen you since the death of the turtle."

As she joined me, Topaz emerged from the kitchen

rolling his eyes. "Mistah Malthus he mad. I's gwan fine Mistah Tom see does he need a boy on his lan. Feet, do yo duty."

Malthus came out of the kitchen with that look on his face that meant something like: Anyone of lesser parts would now be experiencing a very real and justifiable anger; however, my emotions under enviable control, I will now question you quietly and above all, reasonably.

I rose and took him by the arm because reason is a highly combustible material and there were innocent people about. Outside, he blinked, sipped his chateau neuf de pape, and sat down on the cat.

"Arden," he began, re-settling himself, "I'm a reasonable man."

My eye fell on the rabbit barn where a row of dusty bunnies had lined up along the wire fence like a gallery of jurors. "Yes," I admitted, "you have always been nothing if not reasonable."

"I do not mind," he said, "that you have taught the boys to cook. A little haute cuisine becomes a man. Times change and customs change with them."

Amen, I thought.

"But I must tell you that the sight of Arthur in an apron disturbs me."

"Oh, how so?" I asked.

"Arden, your little attempts at guilelessness do not deceive me. You know exactly what you're doing."

I refrained from agreeing.

"You are intent on obliterating all natural distinction between the sexes."

"Malthus," I said, "we were none of us born in aprons."

"And it is precisely that attitude . . ." He had jumped to his feet in vexation and was searching for the internal gear that would re-engage his control system. But the pale blue around his mouth was a dead giveaway. I had gone too far. "It is precisely that attitude which confirms me in my earlier decision. If you're not going to remain in Los Angeles, then I'll seek custody."

Silence slid down like a tired window shade. The bunnies had fallen asleep.

"I'm not a hard man," said Malthus, as if in answer to an accusation. "But children are so Goddamned malleable. They're like clay waiting for the right hand to shape them. Impressionable is what they are."

"Don't flatter yourself," I said. "We are all more or less artists of ourselves."

"Very naive, Arden, very naive." He rocked forward with his hands to his head. The long strand of hair intended to cover his bald spot slipped ever so slightly, revealing a pearl-like luminescence about the size of a baby eggplant atop his head. I smiled.

"To think that you actually believe children grow like weeds in a vacant lot. Arden, that truly makes me afraid for them. Children grow by emulation. When the boys are around me more they'll gradually slough off those effeminate habits they've picked up from your Mr. Topaz Wilson."

"But what if the girls slough off effeminate habits too? What if they emulate your manly gait or from time to time sport moustaches?"

"Don't mock me Arden. They'll emulate Monica, of course."

"That's exactly right," said Topaz, stepping lightly

down the back stairs and holding aloft a tray with a wine decanter and an arsenal of hors d'oeuvres. "They'll all emulate Monica. I'm thinking of emulating Monica myself. Pâté?" he asked, refilling Malthus' glass.

"Mommie, Mommie," said Hillary, careening out the back door, a black olive affixed to the end of each finger. "Oh, hi, Daddy. It's been five hours and the bird still looks funny and Alice don't know what to do."

"Doesn't," corrected Malthus. "Alice *doesn't* know what to do."

Hillary stared.

"Much good it does the children for you to have a Ph.D. in English," said their father.

"I'm a poet," I said, "not a grammarian. I swear to you by the time she's twenty all subject-verb disagreements will have disappeared from her language."

"Miss Arden be right about that," murmured Topaz into the pâté dish, and then in a more audible tone, "So what's the deal with the bird, kid?"

"It's white and sweaty," said Hil. "Alice needs help."

It was the stove, of course. Mrs. Manley, whom I had lovingly named after the first woman to spend the night in jail for her writing, had a heart murmur. Nothing potentially fatal. But she would never again cook at 350 degrees.

I quartered that bird with four quick hacks of the fire axe and threw it on the grill. Kip, who had been the salad boy, I quickly transferred to barbecue chef

— a role I thought Malthus might find more befitting a male — and Alice and I addressed the salad. It was when I gazed up from a pinioned radish that I noticed Ruth noticing Alice.

It seemed to me Ruth might be exceeding her role as Thanksgiving orphan. It seemed Ruth's hunger was perhaps not confined to the prospect of turkey but might be hovering about the potential trimmings.

I threw the remaining radishes in whole, kicked Mrs. Manley in the shins and flung open the back door, platter in hand. Malthus was chatting with his eldest son, who had removed his apron and stuck it in his back pocket.

"Let's eat," I yelled.

"It's not quite done," pronounced Malthus. "Right, son?" He punched Kip in the arm conspiratorially.

"It's done, all right," I said, stabbing the quarters of turkey and flinging them onto the platter.

For once in his life, Malthus was actually right. The joints of the bird were an anguished pink and reminded you uncomfortably that what you were eating had only recently been a living creature with needs and aspirations of his own.

I pretended not to notice and urged a bloody hip on Ruth, who had squeezed in at the table between Alice and me.

"No thank you, Mrs. Malthus," she said. "I really prefer breast."

"I really prefer you not call me Mrs. Malthus," I said, piling my grandmother's enchiladas onto her cranberry sauce. "I no longer fill that position."

"Someone soon will," sang Malthus, with a satisfied glance at Monica, who stared forthwith into her dressing.

"I'm going to be the ring-bearer, Monica says." Hillary glanced at Monica for confirmation.

"I thought boys were ring-bearers. Aren't they?" Malthus glanced about the room like a genial game show host anticipating a correct answer. Malthus likes moments like this when he feigns a reliance on his fellow man and hints at his own possible — but extremely unlikely — fallibility.

"Actually it doesn't matter," said Tom.

Malthus raised his eyebrow. "Have we met?" He was asking to see Tom's credentials.

"I'm Tom," said Tom, who did not understand or chose not to understand that Malthus was preparing to pee on any unidentified turf.

Topaz solved the mystery. "Tom's my lover and the world's florist. He does weddings. For a living."

"Tom's the flower man," laughed Malthus' youngest son.

Malthus stared.

"Who wants pie?" asked Alice, rising with Ruth's plate in her hand.

"You didn't tell me Tom was white," said Malthus next morning through the wire fencing of the rabbit barn. He was on the outside in a three-piece suit and a new toupee. I was on the dim inside in flannel shirt and Levis, feeding three hundred and nine rabbits plus Gloria Bright, the chicken.

"You never asked me what color he was," I said.

"Do you have any idea how all that must have looked yesterday to Monica?"

"What did she say?"

"She didn't say anything."

"Maybe she had a good time. You should ask her."

"Monica doesn't feel obliged to have an opinion about everything. That's one of the really nice things about Monica. She's a lady. If that word means anything to you."

"Less and less," I laughed. Gloria rocked on her grizzled legs and screamed. Most of the visible bunnies fell to eating their greens but two were seized with a sudden ardor and began circling, nuzzling, and biting one another behind the neck.

"It never stops," said Malthus, checking his soles for bunny shit. "You'll have another litter in a few weeks."

"Not from those two, we won't," I said. He looked up, apprehensively. "Males," I confirmed.

"Christ," he exploded and began scraping his feet backward on the gravel, as if he were himself a giant chicken. "Can't we go someplace civilized to have this talk!"

"I didn't realize we were having a talk." I closed the barn door behind me and slid the latch into place.

"Must cost you a fortune," Malthus observed.

"No Malthus, actually they cost you a fortune. I spend the child support on the rabbits; Alice and I pay for the kids ourselves."

"You know," he said, turning against the morning breeze and walking backward, so that his toupee lifted slightly from behind, "you've got an attitude problem."

"Professor Gridley agrees with you," I said.

Malthus held the back door open and motioned me in. While I washed up in the kitchen sink, he sank onto a dining room chair and asked, "So what's the story with the job situation? You planning to stay or what? I need to make some plans."

I told him again. "Malthus, nobody in L.A. is going to hire me because I'm from L.A. They might, later, after I've gone somewhere else and lost my L.A. aura. Then I might be able to come back. But for now I've got to send out the three hundred letters, then wait, and hope for a job interview at the Modern Language Convention in December. It's like playing Bingo, really."

I dried my hands and noticed that Malthus had assumed the position for eliciting pity. He had drawn his knees up, fetus-like, and bent his head to almost touch his knees. Then he opened slowly, like a clam, and pretended to expose his quivering, moist, self.

"You know, Arden, I've always been a good father, even if sometimes I was not the best husband." He turned up slippery eyes to me. I sat down quickly so he'd have to look me straight in the eye. "Those kids are my life," he gasped. "Let me have them, Arden. Or at least the boys."

"That seems fair," said Topaz, coming in from the hall, yawning and heading for the coffee pot. "Thank God, Lillian's replacement has arrived." He pressed his lips to the electric pot then jerked back. "Ouch. Miss Lillian never served me that way. You two want coffee? I'll make more. This has turned to squid ink."

Malthus sat up in his chair and shook his head no to Topaz. "At least think about it. Just the boys."

"That'd be three kids apiece," said Topaz cheerfully. "Y'all ain't gonna get a better deal den dat."

"They're not candy Easter chicks, Malthus, that you can just break apart. And yes, Topaz, I'd love some coffee."

"I've got to get to work," said Malthus. "It's clear we're not going to get anywhere with this ourselves. We'll just have to call in the lawyers."

"Now hold on Malthus," said Topaz, measuring coffee into Lillian's replacement. "How about letting me be the lawyer. I'll be the disinterested party. I've got a real estate license. I could do it."

"You're hardly disinterested." Malthus got up slowly, as if he had a flesh wound his pride prevented him from mentioning.

"Look here," Topaz said, snatching up the kitchen chalkboard and waving it aloft, "you tell me — each of you — what it is you want. I'll write it down. Then we'll see what fits and what doesn't. Simple. Now, Malthus, what do you want?"

Malthus sank back into the kitchen chair. "To influence my children, for God's sake, to mold them with this hand." We all stared at Malthus' hand. It seemed like a bad idea to loose that hand on anybody's children. "And I want to *love* them." Here Malthus dropped his hand, and his head, then finally his shoulders.

"And," he continued in language aimed at the table top, "I am so goddamned tired of paying child support."

Topaz looked at me and I looked at Topaz. Over Malthus' bent head I nodded slowly.

"Malthus, you're exactly right," said Topaz. "All these years you been paying all that money while it's Arden gets the fun of raising those children and not you." He slid into the chair next to Malthus and pulled it closer. "Now what if Arden was willing not to stick it to you anymore? What if she was to climb down off her high horse and say she could get by without that money anymore, provided she got to keep those children?"

"Provided," said Malthus, raising his hand once again, "that they spend every summer with Monica and me."

I nodded again.

"Sold!" said Topaz, letting his hand fall open on the kitchen table.

I could not tell whether striking a bargain with Malthus was another step toward the general breakdown of the universe or the beginning of repair. Still, life seemed to lurch forward again, until one gloomy afternoon early in December when I should have been crouched over my typewriter working on my dissertation. I hated to think of my poems as wheels and cogs in a great functionless machine called *The Dissertation*. Poets had no business delivering a dissertation on anything, any more than professors had any business professing anything. Academicians were a pack of charlatans and lunatics anyway. Then why was I trying to join them?

More and more I felt my interior landscape

clouding over with these rhetorical questions. So, rather than milling out another poem, I was lying in what the children called "Mom's Thinking Hammock" trying to forecast my own life's weather.

I had on my thick Mexican sweater, the one with an entire village woven across the back and breast, with small brown people going about the daily business of being joyous without murdering one another. There was a small child scattering corn on the ground for a circle of appreciative chickens, a grandmother on her knees grinding the corn her grown daughter patted into tortillas and grilled, an old man conversing with his grandson, a man in the distance plowing behind a small gray donkey.

I wanted to claim this scene as my life and to be quietly buried in this very hammock as soon as possible. The thought made me suddenly sit up as straight as was possible in a hammock and earnestly retract this desire. Be-Careful-What-You-Wish was one of my Uncle Ukie's favorite maxims, along with Never-Run-With-a-Kite.

In my imagination I saw my uncle reaching up with his pocket knife to cut the string of his kite, saw the two of us turn and walk toward the kitchen while the kite rose behind us, at first very big, then drifting up and diminishing until it disappeared into the sky like a celestial handkerchief into the divine pocket.

"Please goddess," I said, trying to keep my mind simple and honest, "this was not a wish but a dream vision." I pulled my sweater closer around me.

Then I heard Tom's Austin Healey on the gravel drive. Topaz looked as if the car had been forged around him. Tom leaped out of the driver's seat and

opened the trunk. Topaz opened his door and slowly
unfolded his legs. Neither of my friends had noticed
me watching from the hammock. They were gathering
out of the trunk mysterious dark garments shrouded
in thin plastic bags that fluttered. Tom picked up his
slim fashionable briefcase and they both made for the
back door, laughing like conspirators.

I raised one hand, like a flag, then peeked over
the side.

"There she is, Tom. I told you she'd be a hard
one. And don't tell me you've forgotten, Arden
Benbow!" Topaz stopped in his tracks, then flung the
back of his hand to his mouth and squealed in
dismay. "How would this child ever get a job without
us?" Then he came over to me and leaned down for a
kiss. "Only fourteen more shopping days until the
Modern Language Convention," he reminded gently.

I nodded.

"You'd be surprised what a little costuming can
do," he assured me.

I nodded again.

"Tom understands business."

Then Tom nodded, raising his briefcase by way of
confirmation.

"Nobody," I said, rolling out of my hammock and
following them toward the back door, "ever had such
beauty consultants as you two."

In my bedroom Tom and Topaz began laying out
on the bed various garments from their collection and
from my own closet, which Topaz knew as well as his
own. The briefcase was filled with cosmetics, perfume
bottles, and jewelry.

"First, your undergarments," said Tom, "for they
are the foundation on which our entire impression

must rest. Undergarments are to the human form what primer is to the canvas of a potential masterpiece."

"Which is what you are," said Topaz.

"Indisputably," said Tom, holding up a strange brown wizened object resembling a Voodoo fetish.

"This human masterpiece does not wear panty hose," I said.

"Why not?" said Topaz.

"Have you ever worn pantyhose!" I demanded.

They both stifled a snort of laughter.

"Never mind," I said. "I'll do it." I took off my dreaming sweater and folded it on the bed. Then I unbuckled my overalls; the bib dropped suddenly, dumping onto the floor pencils, tools, change, and a tape measure. "Shit," I said, getting the pant legs stuck on my shoes, which I had forgotten to take off. "After all," I said, "how hard can it be? Right?" By now I was lying on my side, kicking my legs and snarling.

Topaz went to find the ironing board; Tom went to make himself a sandwich.

At last I kicked free of my overalls and jumped to my feet. I stared at the strange fetish lying on the bed. Actually I was no stranger to pantyhose. I had worn them in my working days, my married woman days. First thing in the morning they had always made me feel like my legs were being jammed into my torso. Then by noon the waist would have crept down until it hovered somewhere just above my crotch, while by late afternoon the crotch hovered somewhere just above my knees, rubbing saddle sores into my thighs until at dusk I ripped off the offending garment.

Pantyhose injured not only the body but one's pride.

I picked up from the bed the present pantyhose. Holding their wizened shape up to the light I could see that in five years neither science nor industry had changed them in the slightest. Man might go to the moon, but woman would never rest easily in her pantyhose.

And what was the concept? Women should make their legs look like plastic so as to be less dangerously alluring? Or it might be so they would be more alluring. Or so they would get chronic vaginitis and become distracted from their political goals. The heterosexual mind had always been a puzzle to me.

I snatched the object off the bed and bunched up the first side for its migration up my leg. Flamingo-like, I struck a balance on my left leg, gradually drawing my right foot toward my left knee, and with cautious hands began coaxing my wayward toes toward their appointed destination. Just as I was wondering if anybody had ever written a poem wearing pantyhose, I fell over like a tree in the forest, slowly, gracefully, and without struggle.

Tom and Topaz appeared in the doorway. They were kind enough not to laugh.

After my leg was set and the plaster of Paris almost dry, they told me that the configuration of my body on the floor was a perfect reproduction of the Hanged Man from my mother's Tarot reading. Obviously my journey had begun.

CHAPTER 8:
Happy Birthday to You

"Tell me the truth, Alice," I say, balancing on my cast before the sink and carving rosettes out of radishes. "Do you mind in the least little bit our having to move?"

"Yes, of course I do, dear."

I drop a radish down the sink. Why has she not told me so before? More than two months must have passed since the detonation of Gridley's bomb.

"Why didn't you say so before?" I ask, retrieving the radish.

"You never asked me," she says, deftly cutting crusts off tiny cucumber sandwiches.

"Can't we assume —" I begin.

"Sometimes, Arden, you forget to ask what you don't want to know. You want people's love more than you want the truth."

"Are we having a fight?" I ask.

"Are you having a fight?" asks Arthur, who is nine and seems to be always taking notes for his autobiography.

"Have you and Max finished polishing the shoes?" I ask.

"They're fighting again," screams Arthur, running for the back yard.

"Why do you think we're having a fight," asks Alice, "every time I mention the word 'truth?' Of course I'd rather stay here. I've always loved California. You know that. And now with my promotion at work, I'm finally where I want to be. I'm not answerable to fools and idiots. And quite frankly I like the feeling."

While I stand pondering whether I fall into the category of fool or idiot, a sudden pain streaks down my left leg. My good leg. At precisely the same moment there is a rap on the screen door and my mother's nose comes into view like a photograph in a pan of developing fluid.

"Uuhoo," my mother calls, and bursts through, bearing a large box wrapped in birthday paper. Then my stepfather follows, jingling the change in his pockets, looking vaguely genial.

"My dear," says my mother, circumventing my

nose with hers and nuzzling my neck, "you look terrible." She says this with a look of satisfaction because my mother likes the idea of adversity being in the air but somehow not attaching directly to her. It confirms her world view.

My stepfather, who has no world view, asks me how long I have to wear the cast. People of small imagination prefer data to knowledge. How long, how far, how many, how often?

"Four to six months," says Alice for me.

"And here's the birthday girl," says my mother, hugging Alice to her.

"How old are you, Alice?" asks my stepfather, gathering a little more data.

"Shelden, shame on you," says my mother, sinking deep into our spineless couch. "A lady likes to keep some secrets."

Here she winks at Alice, who promptly says, "Forty-seven."

"Well I know I wouldn't want to tell my age," says my mother, wondering if she has somehow been betrayed.

"I'm six," says Max, crawling into his grandmother's lap and causing her to forgive the world.

"And so you are," she says, kissing his soft neck in the place where he still smells like a baby.

Then Chowder arrives. Chowder is Alice's former husband. He looks and sounds a little like John F. Kennedy so I always have an impulse to fling myself at his feet and beg him to lead the nation out of the abyss into which greed and hypocrisy have plunged it. But it is really all Chowder can do to manage the Department of Water and Power and his own small domestic life. Alice moves forward to kiss Chowder on the cheek, while my mother and stepfather stare — as they always do — in amazement. They cling to the notion that self-respecting heterosexuals ought to despise one another after divorce. I know this is true because my mother always says how wonderful it is that Chowder and Alice can remain friends, while her eyes get that little skeptical squint.

"Let's all sit down," says Alice, looking a bit harassed because seating people is always a problem for us and because I have gone all quiet and she wishes we were not off center in our love, with all this socializing to do. I consider telling a joke to which I remember the punch line but nothing about what leads up to it.

It is at this moment that Ruth arrives, bearing a large, tasteless bouquet of flowers for the birthday girl. She is not wearing her customary sailor suit, but shirt and pants of buttery corduroy that soften her; doubtless Alice's influence. But the sprayed and back-combed coif remains, as well as her red glasses with the little shells glued on. Today is obviously not the day someone will rise, gently remove her glasses, and exclaim, "Why you're beautiful!"

I sit down next to my mother and just let it all happen. Uncle Ukie comes in and pats my knee, saying, "Don't lose your skate key, sport." Aunt Rose, Disney salad chef, is carrying cole slaw in a pale green, nine-foot Tupperware container, which she holds aloft and bears toward the kitchen. Tom, wearing a Basil Rathbone smoking jacket, is chatting at Ruth, his startled and appreciative eyes slowly scaling the heights of her hair; Alice, I notice intrudes herself protectively. Topaz marshals the children into serving lunch on the small paper plates, which after twenty minutes of service begin to go soft and limp. Bruce, the family dog, licks rivulets of cole slaw dressing off the hardwood floor and falls asleep under the dining table.

Over coffee my stepfather tries to convince Uncle Ukie that he needs life insurance, not because he believes my uncle will ever buy any, but because it is Sunday and he hasn't sold anything for almost forty-eight hours. My uncle pronounces the idea a lot of *cangada,* and my stepfather sits back suddenly, knowing and not knowing what *cangada* means. Off in the kitchen I can hear my mother assuring Ruth that we are not Indians but "Early Californians." Alice has just caught Kip trying to light forty-seven candles with the blowtorch from his chemistry set.

The neon pain down my left leg flashes on and off, illuminating dark interior corners.

"You look terrible," repeats my mother, as if my pain has traveled the couch springs from me to her.

"I feel terrible," I admit.

"The leg," says my mother in her best diagnostician's voice.

"No, actually it's the other leg. My good one."

"You haven't got a good one if they both hurt," my mother reasons. "You'd better go to the chiropractor."

My mother refers all illness and injury to the care of chiropractors. Doctors, she believes, make you sick.

"Now promise me," she says.

I suddenly remember the white horse with the red eyes from the Tarot reading my mother gave me last month. My mother rests her hand on my knee as if to remind me the card means change and not death.

When Ukie wanders away from him, my stepfather sits down on the other side of me. "There's no convincing the ignorant," he says, glancing contemptuously in the direction of my uncle, who is now showing Ruth how to lick salt off her wrist before throwing back a shot of tequila.

"That's very true, Shelden," I say, with an emphasis entirely wasted on him.

My mother gets up and heads toward the kitchen because she loves her brother, notwithstanding his stubbornness about life insurance.

"She's a wonderful woman, your mother," pronounces Shelden, who always says this after he has exceeded the boundaries of the decently passive aggressive. "They don't make them like that any more." His eye rests on me as a prime example of the inferior way they make them now. Then he gives a little philosophical shrug as if to dismiss what cannot be and says, "Your mother tells me you gave up your child support. What kind of a deal is that?"

"An expedient one," I reply.

"I thought I taught you better than that."

"You did your best," I assure him.

"You can't live off Alice."

"I'll have a job."

"They're still his kids. He's got to pay. I paid for mine. I didn't like it, but I paid. Asshole," he pronounces.

"I appreciate the sentiment," I say.

"Still, you'll need money. You won't get paid till . . ."

"September, it looks like."

"I don't suppose you've . . ."

"Saved any? No, afraid not."

He runs a thoughtful hand over his delicately shaved baby jaws and says, "I just might be able to throw a little business your way. No promises. But maybe."

"Don't buy any," shouts Uke the Duke from across the room. Upon which the whole house reverberates with song for Alice and her birth.

CHAPTER 9:
Adjustments

Two days later my right index finger rested uneasily on a gaunt and bearded face in the Yellow Pages. The Chiropractor heading came right after Chimney Sweeps and just before Christmas Tree Lights. Aunt Rosie, no stranger herself to imaginary ailments, had recommended Salvador Escobar, whose address she could not remember. There were seventeen pages of chiropractors in the Los Angeles Yellow Pages. In their little yellow photographs they all wore pointed beards and looked malnourished and in pain, except for my mother's Dr. Townsend, who looked like a piece of expensive, yet ill-made upholstered furniture.

His office, I knew, had been done to match in Ethan Allen and there were little plastic boxes about, holding stacks of Christian pamphlets, while for heathen patients there was a table bearing recent copies of *Architectural Digest* and *Sunset*. I had gone there once, at my mother's urging. Actually she had given me a gift certificate after Arthur was born.

Dr. Townsend's assistant had led me down the cranberry carpeting and into an examination room, where she handed me a cotton gown with bunnies on it and barked directions for its assembly through the door closing behind her.

Poised with one arm in the bunny gown, I noticed a chart on the wall not at all in keeping with the lighthearted bunny motifs. It said:

SUBLUXATION LEADS TO A DISORGANIZED
AND UN-CREATIVE EXISTENCE.
SUBLUXATION IMPRISONS AND ENSLAVES.
SUBLUXATION LEADS TO VIOLENCE,
BRUTALITY & EARLY DEATH.

I put on my clothes and left.

I know a curse when I see one. Hence my skeptical feelings now about these bearded young men with pinched eyes. I slammed the Yellow Pages shut. I would find Escobar by intuition and dead reckoning.

Forty minutes later I was stopped at my favorite intersection — the one at Los Feliz and Atwater Avenue — where if your timing is just right you can inhale on a single breath the horses at the Sleepy Hollow Riding Academy, the chlorine from the Los Feliz fountain, and the bears from Griffith Park Zoo. But I wasn't in the right frame of mind to do it. Driving my school bus instead of my Harley-Davidson offered certain impediments. Then there were the wheels and cogs of my mind, churning through the current disasters of my life: my appliances, my lover, my children, my leg, my trip to the MLA Convention, scheduled to happen in just five days. I shifted into first, the clutch setting off a firework display down my left leg, while my right plaster of Paris foot teetered and skidded around on the gas pedal.

I headed down Atwater toward Toonerville. A painful tinsel display of crushed red aluminum flowers swayed overhead. It was going to be another temperatures-in-the-mid-eighties Christmas. I sighed and down-shifted to get a better look at the small businesses crouched along either side of the strèet. Perhaps the goddess would send me on my journey to a place where the look of Christmas squared with all those snow-swept greeting cards of my childhood.

I slammed on the brake with a resounding clunk and grimaced at what I might have done to my right leg. I imagined my ankle and foot as luminous green bones like those you used to see when your mother bought you shoes at Buster Brown and you were left to entertain yourself by sticking your feet into the x-ray machine and training millions of deadly volts of radiation through those impressionable young bones. That's probably why at thirty-seven my bones below the knee were turning to ash and the circuitry in my legs was shorting out.

On the corner was a blue frame house with a sign

in the window that had two fingers pointing in opposite directions: one pointed toward the front door and said "Escobar Chiropractic Clinic" and the other pointed toward infinity — or perhaps only around the corner — and said "Taco Express." My gut, the part of me in charge of art and major decisions, voted — of course — for tacos, while my brain murmured, "But you promised your mother." All arguments were suddenly dispelled by the Pain Express, careening down my spine and making a sharp left at my hips. "All right, all right," I said out loud to the pain-train, "you win."

By then I had overshot the blue house and had to park in the vacuum cleaner repair store, which looked like it was not going to need all its space anyway. I wished I had brought the vacuum cleaner, which had been dead for three days, but how was I to know all my problems might be solved in the same block? I hobbled toward the blue house then up the ramp for the handicapped and paused at the front room window. There was a tiny Christmas tree with a surgical cotton skirt tucked around its feet and three million candle-shaped lights with boiling liquid in them. I had not seen lights like that since my grandmother died.

Suddenly the door opened, and then just as suddenly was pulled almost shut again. A woman's voice said, "*Padrecito,* I told you I would open the door."

And then a man's voice said, "I think I may open my door as long as God gives me strength. I was only sitting and speaking with the dog."

Then the door popped open on an elderly man wearing a plaid flannel shirt, baggy corduroy trousers, and his house slippers. Behind him was a beautiful dark young woman, with a gap between her front teeth, and miniature Christmas balls dangling from her ears. Her nose was beyond expression. I stared. "I don't have an appointment," I said, as if I had come precisely to tell them they had no time for me.

But one of them flung the door open and they moved about in the small room to make room for me. There were four unmatched stuffed chairs competing for space, empty except for the one occupied by a huge brown poodle with a gray muzzle about the shade of Dr. Escobar's own poodley locks. Opposite the dog stood a skeleton with his left arm raised and a finger pointing in the general direction of Taco Express or infinity, whichever occurred first.

"I keep the dog," said Dr. Escobar, "for a friend."

"Emilio is dead," his daughter gently reminded.

I looked in the direction of the skeleton.

"Emilio is buried in Forest Lawn," she said, as if to convince her father and head off any speculation on my part. "In Slumbering Gardens."

"And yet I keep his dog," the old man replied, as if presenting the last word on the matter. "The dog of my friend Emilio."

The dog looked up suddenly, regarded us all with a mildly critical eye, then yawned, resettled his big head, and fell asleep.

"He is very old," observed the young woman, as if life sometimes threatened to exceed her control. "But what can my father do for you?" She held out to him a white, starched jacket that she had taken from the elk horns next to the fiberboard fireplace.

"But I'm not cold," he said.

"You look more professional."

"I don't gain knowledge with a coat," he said, looking at me. "Do I?"

"Well I never have," I said, not wanting to contradict the beautiful, fine-nosed daughter.

"*Bueno.* You come with me, young woman, and Maria Jesus, that's enough foolishness."

"It's the twentieth century," she said, returning the jacket to the elk horns.

"*Sí, sí,*" he said, leading me down a dim hall, past a bedroom with the door ajar. "And one day, if God permits, we will have the twenty-first century and still a white coat will not give me wisdom. Or you either, *mi hija.*"

He flipped on the light. In the center of the room was an upholstered table with a clean white sheet. Along one wall, the pink wall, ran a counter with various medical implements, and in the middle of the blue wall a small window looked out on what might be a used car lot. Along an orange wall lounged an old couch with a moss-green cover thrown over what must have been its more historical parts. In the corner was an ancient wooden file cabinet and on top of it a skull.

Beautiful daughter came in and unrolled some paper onto the table — which the father removed — and went to the window and drew closed white curtains with green cactuses printed all over them. Then she took a clipboard off the counter and handed it to me.

"*El teléfono,*" said Dr. Escobar to his daughter. "It calls. I can manage here without you." When she was gone he took the clipboard from my hand and motioned toward the couch. I sank deep into

whatever the moss-green cover covered and felt the
pain zip from hip to arch.

Dr. Escobar leaned forward and tapped gently on
my cast. "This is not the problem. It must be the
other one. From bearing the burden, you see. After I
fix you, you must walk with a cane for a time. Not
crutches. They misalign."

"Subluxation?" I asked. "Violence, brutality and
early death?"

He laughed. "Pain, yes, certainly," he agreed.
"But as for early death, there simply is no such
thing. *No existe*. Study *la calavera*, not the men in
white jackets. What do men in white jackets know?"

I looked at the skull. I looked and remembered my
Aunt Vi and how she had that summer in Mexico
insisted I visit with her the mummies of Guanajuato.
Maybe I had not looked long enough or well enough.
Images of death had certainly crawled, cantered, and
marched across my field of vision ever since my
mother had flung down the Death card in my Tarot
reading. What did the goddess have in mind for me? I
looked into Dr. Escobar's river-brown eyes.

"You'll be all right," he said, and patted my knee.
I gulped air and felt like a large, ancient poodle.

Twenty minutes later I was following the arrow
around the blue house toward Taco Express. I felt six
inches taller and my good leg was good again. My
back felt curiously straight and I could almost feel
the blood coursing cheerily along its conduits,
overpasses, and clover leafs, passing again through

territories that had become ghost towns of my circulatory system.

Taco Express, it turned out, was part of Dr. Escobar's chiropractic office, and the house itself was scattered through both. I was scanning the hand-lettered menu over the grill when Maria Jesus suddenly appeared behind the counter as if shot from a cannon. She was tying a clean apron over her clean medical assistant's dress. I didn't know whether or not to pretend I'd never seen her before.

I remembered a cheap circus my father had taken me to years and years ago when I had recognized the lady on the elephant as the aerialist from twenty minutes before and the clown from forty minutes before. My father had told me to pretend they were different people. That seemed easier than thinking of them as one.

I looked at Maria Jesus now with admiring eyes. I almost told her she had a wonderful nose. Instead I ordered two chicken flautas and thumped over to the nearest yellow and blue picnic table. While Maria Jesus set up a cloud of fragrant grease, I imagined myself in white silk pajamas astride an elephant, playing celestial flute music to Maria Jesus on the high wire. Getting my subluxation straightened out had done funny things to my brain.

By the time she slid the flautas to me on a paper plate I was feeling faintly adulterous. Alice tells me these seizures are the aftermath of my Catholic upbringing, vague as that had been.

My father had been an atheist with a burning — one might almost say an anthropological interest in Catholicism — while my mother only went to mass on Easter, though with great regularity, as if — like an American living abroad too long — she might, if she were careless, lose her Vatican citizenship. So it was my father who took me to mass when at the age of eight a brief though ardent religious fervor suddenly overcame me. But it was difficult to take most of the mysteries seriously, sitting next to a straight-backed father glancing around with genteel curiosity while the faithful knelt, moaned, and struck their breasts in contrition.

My father's attitude has probably worked its way into various synapses in the left side of my brain, but still a few Catholic terrors flicker from time to time through the right. I suppose I prize them for their clarity. One of these is the belief that imagining a sin is the same as actually committing it. As a child I was so good at imaginary sin that I did not realize until I was a grownup that if thinking the sin was as bad as doing the sin, then you might as well go ahead and have the pleasure of action and not just imagination. Poets tend to be devious, though. And Alice, for one, is beginning to lose patience with lapsed Catholics.

I decided in her honor to simply give myself up to this order of flautas Maria had set before me, and to sink my teeth into that crunchy, faintly bacon-flavored, warm and yielding chicken breast enfolded in a tortilla, with all the poetic license in the world.

A male youth with slicked back black hair took the bench opposite me. He leaned forward. "Enrique," he said.

"I beg your pardon?" I said through my flauta.

"Enrique. But you can call me Chavo. I'm in

transportation." He spun on the bench and threw out his right hand, like a tap dancer come to rest. In the direction he indicated were six or seven cars pulled up at the back of the lot next to the blue house. Across the front, green flags fluttered. A banner proclaimed WHEELS BY ENRIQUE.

"Maria tells me you need transportation."

"I have transportation already, Enrique." I looked toward the counter but Maria had disappeared. Maria was an entrepreneur, it seemed. I resolved not to fall in love with strangers ever again.

"Chavo," he reminded gently. "So what are you driving?"

"A nineteen-fifty-three GMC school bus."

"No kidding!" Chavo whacked his bullfighter thigh at that one, rolled back, then forward, to stop, eyes wide before me.

"Really," I said, gathering my paper products for a getaway.

"Wait a minute, waitaminute." Chavo put his hand on my forearm. "Maria says you got subluxation bad. You want one comfortable vehicle. Am I right? I got a cream puff with your name on it. This one's hot."

"Hot?" I said.

"No, no, nothing like that. I mean cool, man. I mean this is one fine short."

"Short wouldn't do. I've got six kids, Chavo. I have strange needs where transportation is concerned." I rose, clutching my empty plate as if it were a steering wheel.

"Jesus Christ," he said. "Look at that leg."

I looked at my leg.

"I bet you got manual shift too. Seven gears on

that baby. You going to have subluxation forever, man. No way."

I made it to the trash container.

"Listen," said Chavo, lifting the trash lid. "I got the perfect solution for you."

"There is no perfect solution for me, Enrique."

"Now there's your problem. You're too negative, man. You got to think positive. Maria taught me that. Maria tells me, Chavo, she says, you never going to get anywhere with that kinda attitude. You got to think positive."

Maybe Maria was right. Her father did not think she was right about much of anything. But how could anybody with a nose like that be substantially wrong? I would listen.

Chavo must have sensed a change in my body language. He slid his hand under my arm and we hobbled toward the vacuum repair store, the youth whispering incantations into my ear. "Automatic transmission, AC, automatic windows, electric locks, tinted windows . . ."

At the bus he stopped, slid himself underneath, came out with a smear of oil on his cheek and a smile on his face. "That baby's seen a lot of hard times."

"And good ones," I said.

He lifted the hood and looked at the engine. "This baby's never going to leave Toonerville," he prophesied. "But I know a dude who'd give you three hundred dollars for it."

"Three hundred dollars! It's worth twice that."

"Three hundred would be generous. But let me tell you the deal I'm cooking for you. How'd you like to have a Cadillac?"

"A Cadillac!"

"One thing I know," said Chavo, opening out his hand and pointing into his palm with deliberation, as if the one thing he knew were inscribed there. "Everyone wants a Cadillac."

"Not this one."

"Everybody wants a Cadillac. Deep down inside, I mean. Deep."

I quickly scanned my subconscious for the buried Cadillac.

"And then it's practical."

I laughed.

He took my forearm again. "For you it's practical. You got six kids. This baby can seat nine. More than nine with those little fold-out seats! This baby's fully loaded."

"How can it seat nine people? It must be a limousine."

"You could call it that," said Chavo, looking off toward the dying Christmas decorations.

After dinner that night I called everybody outside to acknowledge the Cadillac inside them and appreciate the one resting in their driveway.

"It looks like a car for dead people," said Max.

"It *is* a car for dead people," said Topaz.

"It's a limousine," I said.

Alice stared.

101

BOOK II

CHAPTER 10:
Time's Wingéd Chariot

"I'm almost fifty," Alice said, setting my dissertation atop my Minnie Mouse underpants and snapping shut the jaws of Ruth's blue Samsonite.

"You just turned forty-seven," I said. "I distinctly remember your birthday party. Four days ago you turned forty-seven." I picked up the suitcase experimentally in my right hand, Aunt Vi's cane in my left, and lumbered about the room in my cast.

"Did you pack your crêpe de Chine blouse?" asked Topaz, sticking his head through the bedroom door.

"That's easy for you to say," observed Alice.

"Actually it was," said Topaz. "I just opened my mouth and out it slid."

"I mean Arden," said Alice. "It's easy to say forty-seven is not old when you're not even forty yet."

"Almost," I said. "Forty is imminent."

"Thirty-eight is imminent."

Topaz retreated, murmuring, "And always at my back I hear, Time's wingéd chariot hurrying near."

"I do hear it. That's exactly what I hear."

"Probably because of the hearse," I said. "I should never have bought it."

"I thought it was a limzine," piped a voice from down the hall. "You said it was a limzine."

I dropped Ruth's suitcase and Aunt Vi's cane and took Alice in my arms. We both cried a little and then laughed.

"It's your having to leave," said Alice, "so soon after Christmas. It seems so barbaric to have this MLA thing the day after Christmas. What kind of people must they be?"

"What kind, indeed," I said, nibbling her ear.

"Well, at least you'll see Ruby."

"Yes, Ruby," I said, sitting down on the bed. "Now think about Ruby. She must be in her seventies and still going strong."

"Seventy-four," said Alice, "but who's counting. I hope I have her courage when I'm her age. Selling her trailer park, that was risky."

"Adventuresome," I said, remembering I had not

packed my overalls. I hobbled around to my closet and found Topaz in there taking inventory.

"That's easy for you to say," called Alice. "That was her retirement money."

"Where's the crêpe de Chine blouse?" Topaz asked. "The one Ruth is lending you."

"You mean polyester."

"Yes, but if I called it that you wouldn't wear it."

"I hate polyester. It gives off sparks."

"Electric personality," said Topaz. "Now where the hell is it?"

"I don't think I'd be willing to do that," said Alice from the bedroom.

"Wear polyester? Me neither. It's flammable."

"Give up my retirement."

I handed Topaz the offending garment, whereupon it slid off its wire hanger to the floor. "Watch out," I said. "Ten thousand volts." I hopped into the bedroom with my overalls.

"I suppose buying the catering business with Honey can be considered a reinvestment, but at seventy, to risk every cent she's ever made —"

I snapped open the Samsonite and stuffed my overalls in, then eased myself onto the bed next to Alice, trying not to disturb her train of thought. We both lay quiet, listening to the sound of hangers.

"I like to think of Ruby on her swing," I said at last.

"I don't," said Alice. "Stripping for a bunch of drunken wartime sailors must have been demeaning."

"Actually, she says not. She used to talk about those times with Aunt Vi. In her trailer park. Ruby's Campground and Trailer Park. We'd sit outside at night. Warm Guaymas nights. She'd tell about Ruby Red from Frisco, Girl on the Red Swing. I can hear her voice in the night, rough and tender."

Alice picked up my hand and kissed it. "I almost wish I were going."

"And I wish this crêpe de Chine were going," said Topaz, bearing toward the suitcase a small, neatly folded stack of Ruth Sharp's best clothes.

"You will need some clothes that won't wrinkle," said Alice, lifting the lid. "You tend to go about wrinkled."

"I distrust whatever is incapable of acquiring wrinkles, whether in clothes or people," I said, kissing Alice softly.

I would be lying if I said I had no misgivings as I handed over Ruth's two blue Samsonite bags to the unwashed man impersonating a TWA curbside baggage handler. He had the eyes of an ax murderer, so I did not question him but hobbled through the pneumatic doors.

It was impossible not to think of doors, as these shut behind me. How many doors had I been through since the alarm went off this morning at 5:40? Not counting the bathroom door there had been . . . I eased myself onto a plastic chair to count . . . fourteen. Of course some of these I counted twice because I had gone through them both ways, but there was definitely a pattern here. Doors were beginnings and endings. Through them the same person could not pass — come to think of it — twice. Because the person would be different on the return trip. Even the door would be different, having sloughed off or rearranged some of its molecules and door atoms.

I watched people hurrying to catch their planes, not pausing to contemplate the significance of doors. Was this what full-time permanent employment meant? That one had no time to run inquiring hands lovingly over life's metaphors? If I succeeded at deluding these MLA people into seeing me as an employable person, would I then become one?

Not since Malthus had anyone tried to exert such power of definition over me. I felt as if someone had by stealth slipped a plastic dry-cleaning bag over my face and body, tying me off with a giant twistum around the ankles. I stood, gasping, weaving, wanting to catch sight of myself in a smeary public mirror to see if I looked any different since 5:40 this morning.

"Watch it," said an old lady in black old-lady shoes as our canes collided. She stared at my cast and then looked up into my eyes as if I were an escaped lunatic. "People like you," she said.

I went to the rest room. The one with the silhouette of a woman in a dress. "I have a dress," I murmured, bursting through the door, arm outstretched, and nearly karate chopping a sullen-looking teenager trying to exit.

"Jeez," she said, eloquently.

"Jeez," I replied, and turned into the diaper-changing room. In the smeary full-length mirror I studied myself. My hair hung straight and dark, emphasizing my long narrow face. My Indian face. My eyes were black as olives. They glowered. I was wearing a polyester bell-bottom slack suit my mother had given me so that I might look "professional." It was the exact color of a maraschino cherry. Topaz had tied one of Tom's scarves at the throat to pacify me. One foot sported my cast, which Alice had lovingly painted white the night before so that none of the epigraphs would prove offensive to the powerful, and the other featured a new brown lizard-skin pump belonging to Ruth. I felt more kinship with the lizard than with Ruth.

Somehow her clothes, accessories, and accouterments seemed to dominate my wardrobe, but it was clear from the Snow White mirror's account that they would never overcome my fierce eyes and warrior spirit. I picked up Alice's purse and Ruth's blue Samsonite make-up case in my left hand and Aunt Vi's cane in my right, then lifted the cane in tribute to the image in the mirror. The young mother careening through the door with a baby under her arm gasped.

"Hi," I said, "I've got six," and strode out the seventeenth door of the day.

When I got to the proper gate everybody else had boarded TWA Flight 34 to San Francisco. A man in a stiff white shirt with wings on it said he was sorry. I showed him my ticket. He spoke at some length on the subjects of punctuality and responsibility. That failing, he spoke about fate. Not well, but I appreciated the effort.

Then he looked deep into the computer. There was after all a charter flight leaving from Panacea Airways in an hour.

"Panacea?" I said. Somehow I always seemed to fly airlines with names that suggested the ephemeral or the chimerical.

"You'll like Panacea," he said genially. "It's a great little airline."

"Define *little*," I said.

He laughed and marked on my ticket with a grease pen.

Of course Panacea left from a different terminal.

LAX is designed around a circle, I knew. Theoretically if you caught an airport bus and stayed on it, eventually you must arrive at your airline.

There was no time to explore the metaphor. I boarded a bus and rode it three times around the smoggy circle, balancing myself uneasily between Ruth's blue Samsonite overnight case and Aunt Vi's cane. Finally I asked the driver.

"Jou want Air Fright," he told me. "Of the jello bus."

The yellow bus was smaller and smelled of diesel. We left the circle and followed a rutted road out to a cluster of three rusting hangars. I was relieved to see that Air Fright was housed in its own hangar; next to that was Cornucopia Air, and then Panacea. Considering the other two alternatives, I supposed I had done all right.

People were queuing up at gate three, the only gate in the building. Over their heads stretched a plastic banner that said in huge turquoise and yellow letters: WELCOME TO PANACEA, THE PARTY AIRLINE. I wondered vaguely if it was too late to opt for Air Fright.

"You must be Teddy LaRue," said a young woman in a tight-fitting black dress over which she wore a tiny turquoise apron that said PANACEA.

"Arden Benbow," I said.

111

She laughed and pinned Teddy LaRue's name tag on my mother's leisure suit. Then she waved gaily to another young woman in black dress and apron who stood at the head of the line. "Teddy's here," she called above the chatter and laughter. "It's Teddy."

"Listen —" I began, as the ragged line lurched through the gate toward the waiting plane.

I settled myself painfully into Teddy LaRue's aisle seat. Ruth's blue cosmetic case would not quite fit under the seat in front of me, and Aunt Vi's cane rolled into the aisle and tripped Grace Bombadil from Thousand Oaks, who then careened into the young woman in the turquoise Panacea apron. The young woman — to her credit — did not lose her cool but glanced quickly at Grace Bombadil's seating assignment and hoisted her bodily into the aisle seat opposite. Then she bent to pin my name tag on me.

Vapors of Arpege, blended delicately with body odors as warm and musky as fresh baked bread, rose from her breastworks. I sat very still. I have a dentist like this: he touches you so lightly you're not sure he's touching you.

"There," she said, pressing into my knees as Grace Bombadil motored past on her way to the john.

"There," I answered.

"I'm glad you could make it," she said with a smile.

As she moved forward in the cabin, bending and dispensing tiny white pillows as if they were Communion wafers, I stared down at my name tag. TEDDY LaRUE it said, and there were three long-stemmed roses made of Tupperware stapled to the shining card.

I let my tired head fall back on the Panacea logo and my chin rest on the Tupperware roses. The engines whined irritatingly, the body of the plane groaned forward, and Grace Bombadil whisked into her seat on a cloud of diesel fumes, telling me, en route, that she was Grace Bombadil.

"Teddie LaRue," I said, taking her angel food hand. "Sorry about the cane."

"When you travel," she said with a twinkle, "you're entitled to raise a little Cain."

Teddie smirked in complicity.

Clearly Teddie was not Catholic. I rather liked her for that. Her soul was an example of open architecture, while mine tended to have a few doors giving off the living room, and even a lumber room or two up in the attic where unlabeled boxes were stored. I thought of Jane Eyre and Thornfield Hall, of fluttering candles in dark hallways, of Mrs. Rochester's mad laughter.

Obviously I had read too much Victorian fiction in my life. Teddie LaRue, however, read *Cosmo*, took tests in ladies' magazines, and did not much trouble herself when she flunked them.

I resolved once more to give up calling plain, healthy, appreciative responses thought-sin. But wasn't that yet another symptom of survivors of childhood Catholicism? They were always giving up something.

My friend Cocoa Kirby says the problem with resolutions is they're too hard to keep. She makes resolutions that are easy and pleasant. Like: Buy more shoes.

I reached up and touched the black linen elbow of the Panacea flight attendant. "I'm afraid I didn't catch your name," I said.

"Bunkie Parker," she said, sliding her hand into mine unnecessarily. "Fasten your seat belt."

An hour later I stood by Panacea's moving conveyer belt waving good-bye to Bunkie Parker and my sister Tupperware salespeople. They would see me back at the hotel, they'd said, waving gaily. Bunkie was catching a ride with them to the hotel because, as she explained to me with what is described in fiction as "a meaningful look," she had a three-day layover in San Francisco.

My luggage, on the other hand, was resolutely on its way to Seattle.

I stepped outside to wait for Ruby. The Panacea Airlines plate glass window rattled in its casing. From here the main terminal looked like a reclining animal, nursing its young; planes attached somehow near the mouth sucked passengers into warm bellies. Turbo-sighs wafted in. Beyond the terminal lolled the Pacific, little glints of light playing off her surface and striking down deep toward the dozing fish.

Off in the distance I could see a white van moving my way, dipping and bouncing along bleached asphalt. "I'm a poet," I said out loud, then reached down for the suitcase handle, my hand passing through air, my cane sliding out of the other hand and bouncing on the sidewalk. Then there were van doors popping open and engulfing hugs from Ruby, from Honey, my dear old friends.

"Jesus," said Ruby, "it took you long enough. Damned airlines. Pure piracy. And look at you. Tired as a dog." She hugged me again.

"What happened to your foot?" said Allison Honey, bending close, her honey-blonde hair falling across her face.

"Look like you were dragged through a damned rat hole," said Ruby gently. "Where's your luggage?"

"In Seattle," I said.

"Here," said Ruby, sliding open the van door. "You ride in back with the cake. You got time to change before you go conventioning?"

I crawled in next to a chocolate cake made up of six or eight thin layers and crowned with the words HIRE A POET. It had two sandbags holding the plate steady. I settled into a red, futon-like thing next to it.

"Great-looking cake, Honey." I blew her a kiss.

Ruby was driving. She had a headband tied across her forehead and gray wirey hair sticking up over the top like healthy rosemary. She wore jeans and a faded work shirt that said GRAY PANTHERS across her back in cross-stitch. I hadn't seen her since Alice and I got married in the back yard five years ago. She had gained weight since the wedding, but the extra pounds looked like football padding over her chest and back. She wore bright red lipstick that made her mouth look like dime store wax lips. And how I loved her!

Honey wore some kind of flowing sari-like thing of rumpled cotton, blues and purples all running into each other. She had the kind of hair princesses let down out of tower windows till they finally wised up.

I tugged at my mother's maraschino-red polyester leisure suit. "I wish I could change," I said.

115

"We're all changing, Arden," said Honey, smiling softly from the front seat.

"My clothes, I mean."

"Oh," said Honey, sitting upright. "I thought you meant your life."

"Lycra," I said, snapping the material over my thighs.

"I feel driven to a pun," said Ruby, snorting to herself and letting the clutch chatter as she pulled onto the Bayway. "Lycra or not."

Honey and I groaned.

"Privilege of age," said Ruby.

"Your whole life is a privilege of age," I said. "For example, if I were you instead of me I would not be going to the slave block at the MLA convention this very minute."

"No," said Ruby, "you'd be driving a catering truck."

"Happily," I said.

"If you feel that way," said Honey, "then why go?"

"I'm not sure," I said, studying the motto on the cake. "It all seems to have begun with Dr. Gridley's observation that it was time."

"That Gridley," said Honey. "She meddles in people's lives too much. Remember when she told me I was not Ph.D. material after the rabbits ate my paper on Henry James? She had no right."

"No," said Ruby, "she didn't. But if she hadn't said that, you might be going to the block right along with Arden here, instead of riding around in a catering truck with this swell old Jane."

"You mean you two . . ."

"It happened right after the wedding," said Honey, her face alight. "Maurio and Michael drove us up the coast afterwards. Ruby and I were right back where you are now."

"Except there was no red mattress like you got," laughed Ruby.

"We talked," said Honey. "Ruby told me her life story and I fell in love with it."

"I fell in love with possibility," said Ruby, wiping under her sunglasses. "And then we just both goddamned well fell in love with each other, and still are, if I may speak for Honey here."

I crawled up between them and hugged them both hard, trying not to sob. I felt such relief and didn't know why. I wished Aunt Vi were here instead of in that gaudy crypt in Forest Lawn where Uncle Groot insisted on putting her instead of letting us provide for her an Indian burial in Guanajuato that summer, as she would have wished.

"Christ I miss Vi," said Ruby, as if she had read my mind. "I wish she was sitting with you right now back there and telling your fortune with those cards of hers. Remember? The Queen of Cups," said Ruby, glancing dangerously over the driver's seat in my direction. "That's what Vi used to call you. Those were sweet times. Christ, yes."

"Sweetheart, it makes me nervous when you're driving and rolling your eyes up like that. You can't be watching the road," observed Honey. "And where are we going, anyway?"

"The Mark Hopkins," I groaned.

Ruby made a sudden right, almost flinging me into the cake.

117

"I have an idea," said Honey, as if the sudden change of direction had jostled her brain into creativity. "Let's trade clothes."

I eyed her flowing tie-dyes. They looked comfortable.

"Here, she said, slipping between the front seats and skirting the cake. "Let's swap."

We rolled around on the futon like circus clowns until at last she was in the firm grip of my mother's leisure suit and one of Ruth's alligator pumps and I was clad in blue cotton and one earth sandal.

In front of the Mark Hopkins, Ruby slid the van door open, and I stepped out into a circle of Tupperware conventioneers, all of whom squealed — to Ruby's delight — "Teddy LaRue! Teddie's back!"

At the registration desk Professor Saltmarsh disavowed any knowledge of my existence. I was standing in the A to F line in the lobby of the Mark Hopkins. She kept running her mechanical pencil up and down the print-out sheets and shaking her head. Each time she looked up at me her dubious expression notched up in the direction of pure suspicion. She was twenty-four if she was a day and I began to understand Alice's sense of panic. Others had lead more orderly lives than ours. They had already scrambled half-way up the magic mountain while far beneath them, we had just rolled into the parking lot. I felt like some kind of ethnic curiosity, standing there in Honey's rumpled tie-dyed dress, one foot in a cast, the other in an earth sandal, Ruth's blue Samsonite cosmetic case resting on the Mark

Hopkins' oriental rug, Aunt Vi's cane propped against Professor Saltmarsh's mahogany library table.

"Well, do you have your receipt? You ought to have a receipt."

The receipt was in the left upper pocket of my mother's maraschino leisure suit which now graced Honey's body.

"I lost my luggage," I said. "It's in Seattle. All my medication was in there." I gave Professor Saltmarsh my half-mad leer and let my head tremble ever so slightly.

She typed out a name tag, slipped it into a plastic sheath, and handed it to me forthwith. "Wear this," she said, "to *all* MLA functions."

"You'll never regret this," I said, gathering up my cane and cosmetic case and hobbling toward the French doors that said, MESSAGES.

Professor Gridley had explained to me painstakingly the importance of the message boards. "Particularly in your case," she had appended.

She referred to the fact that I had only two scheduled interviews, despite the three hundred letters that my son Kip had lovingly typed at twelve cents a letter.

"It suggests — does it not? — that the market for poets is not quite what it should be." Then she made that detestable little hamster sound that was her laugh. "So the message board will be your lifeline. Schools that have not set up their interview schedule may ask to see you. They won't trouble with the phone because the switchboard will be quite impossible. Job candidates trying to get through. Futile, of course, quite futile." She snorted with ironic compassion. "Oh, and Benbow, a name tag at

119

all times." She knew, it seemed, several people who had been hired out of elevators.

I paused now to attach my name tag. I was nothing if not obedient.

"Teddie?" came a voice at my left elbow. "Teddie, can that possibly be you?"

It was Bunkie, in a shimmery golden blouse and a black skirt, standing next to a woman in a dusty-rose tuxedo. I had always dreamed of a dusty-rose tuxedo.

"Stash," said Bunkie to the tuxedo in question, "this is Teddy, remember? From the plane. Teddie, this is my friend Stash."

We shook hands and stared at each other.

"We're going dancing," said Bunkie. "We'd love it if you could come."

Stash nodded agreement. Stash had short hair, very short about the ears and neck, where it was gray, then longer as it grew out and up into a kind of auburn triangle. It was an astonishing piece of topiary. I had an impulse to touch the top of it.

"I've got to work," I said. "Otherwise I'd like to."

"What do you do, Teddie?" Stash asked amiably.

"Tupperware," Bunkie answered. "Teddie's in Tupperware."

"So," said Ruby that evening, plunging an enormous chef's knife deep into the chocolate cake, "what's the scoop on this Teddie Whatsername?"

We sat on bright futons on the hardwood floor. Ruby had explained that because Honey could not meditate with furniture in the room, they had donated it to Gaywill. I was wearing Ruby's baseball pants and an oversized sweatshirt faded to the color of ancient wine. Across the chest in dim silver letters it said AGED TO PERFECTION.

"That's me," I said, reaching out for the first slice. "Teddie LaRue. Apparently I'm in Tupperware."

"You lead a complicated life," observed Honey. "I'm trying to follow Henry David Thoreau's advice and simplify my life."

I looked at Ruby. She smiled and handed Honey a slice of cake. "Simple is nice," she said. "But crazy is nice too, I got to admit."

"Well, just look," said Honey, raising up one slim hand to count on. "First, she's Arden Benbow. Right? But she arrives wearing her mother's suit, a scarf belonging to somebody named Tom, carrying Aunt Vi's cane, and Alice's purse. The luggage of a party named Ruth has gone on to Seattle without her. Now phone calls from people named Muffie for somebody named Teddie, who is really Arden." I stared. She was right. My identity had taken on the texture and substance of Play Doh. I stared at my plastic fork. The room was so silent for a moment that you could hear the cat purring.

"Yes," said Ruby, picking up the cat and placing her like a boa around her pink neck. "And she wears Minnie Mouse underpants — if my eyesight hasn't failed me — and yet I don't think we could call her Minnie Mouse."

"I really wouldn't object," I said. "After Teddie, why draw the line?"

"Your Aunt Vi was like that," said Ruby. "Always giving people new names. Like Maurio, for example. I can't even remember his real name."

"How are Maurio and Michael? I haven't seen them since the wedding."

"It's depressing," said Honey.

"It's change," said Ruby. "That's all."

"Then I hate change," said Honey mildly.

"So do I. Tell me what happened."

"We don't really know what happened," said Ruby, releasing the cat.

"Yes we do. They stopped loving each other," said Honey. "Maurio started fooling around with a sword-swallower or something. They sold us the catering business. Michael moved away."

"That doesn't mean," said Ruby, "that they don't love each other."

"I don't understand you, Ruby. What else could it mean?"

"Don't ask me," said Ruby, reaching for the plates. "I'm a simple baker. But I can tell you I've never stopped loving anybody in my life."

"Me either," I said, evening up the cake with the giant knife. "I'm still in love with Jane Oliver, for instance."

"Who's Jane Oliver?" they both asked.

"Oh," I said with a laugh, "that was a long time ago. When I got my ears pierced. In Iowa."

"Iowa!"

"Malthus was working on his MBA and we were living in married-student housing. In a Quonset hut. Kip and Jamie were just babies. Jane lived at the other end with her husband and baby. Beyond a wall as thin as a membrane. You could hear people breathe through it. One day I saw her sitting under the clothesline reading Virginia Woolf. Diapers were flapping about her head. I fell in love."

"What about the pierced ears?" Honey prompted.

"Well I never had them pierced when I was a baby. My reasonable father always said I should be baptized and get my ears pierced, or not, as I saw fit when I reached the age of reason. I tend to delay decisions."

"So . . ."

"So, when we had to leave, Malthus and I, I had my ears pierced in hopes a tiny pain would keep me from noticing the pain of my heart breaking."

"And . . ."

"There wasn't any 'and.' "

"You never . . ."

"We shook hands," I said, suppressing a sob.

"My God," said Honey. "And I guess you didn't get baptized either."

"Honey," said Ruby, with a sharp look.

"I just wondered."

The phone rang when Honey leaned forward to kiss Ruby.

"Alice. My God I forgot to call her."

"It might be that Bunkie person again. Take it in our room. Next to the bed."

A voice from underwater identified itself as the Long Distance Operator. She had a person-to-person for an Arden Benbow. Was I an Arden Benbow?

"Arden, Arden," came the tiny voice of my beloved.

"Alice, is that you?"

"Are you Miss Benbow?" insisted the underwater operator.

"Certainly," I said. "I am she."

"Go ahead plea-uz."

"Dear," said Alice, "you were going to call."

I flopped back onto the warm waterbed, then undulated. "It's good to hear your voice. Seems like six weeks."

"How's it going?"

"I have arrived. My luggage is in Seattle. Ruby and Honey are feeding me cake. I am having an identity crisis. All my clothes belong to other people. Mostly to Ruth."

"You are not the sum total of the outfits you wear," said my Alice. "Naked you came into the world."

"Very true," I said. "And I may have to go about that way tomorrow. Or wear Ruby's baseball pants." I sat up and studied the grass-stained knees.

"They'll think you're a lesbian," said Alice.

"I *am* a lesbian," I said.

"You won't want them to think so just yet, dear. It's not politic. Not if you're serious about getting a job."

"Gridley is serious. I'm not."

"I think you are," said Alice quietly.

CHAPTER 11:
Beyond Tupperware

"So much for simplicity," said Honey in the van next morning as she straightened my MLA name tag and brushed cat hair off the expensive suit borrowed from their next-door neighbor the night before, a lawyer whose garments exuded success. I rose unsteadily and picked up her empty briefcase. Ruby ran around to open the door for me. I tried to feel like a paratrooper over enemy territory, but I felt more like a confection that my caterer friends were delivering to the Mark Hopkins kitchen. I stuck my head out, alert for Tupperware salespeople up early.

"Break a leg," Ruby said gaily, then looked down at my cast. "Should have cut that off last night. The cast, I mean. Ruins the effect."

"Thanks anyway," I said, taking Aunt Vi's cane from Honey.

They crushed me in a group hug and released me to the Modern Language Association.

Inside, the hotel was dark and cushioned. A few academics lounged in big leather chairs holding the *New York Times* between their faces and whatever life might unaccountably offer. I was early. My appointment with Midway College was at 9:00 a.m. It was 8:45. I would go to the coffee shop, then to the message board, then it would be time.

In the doorway to the coffee shop, I spotted a hand fluttering beneath a large hanging fern. It belonged to Grace Bombadil from the plane. Momentarily I feigned nearsightedness, then relented and made my way to her booth where she was patting the naugahyde in welcome.

"Teddie," she said, "I've been looking all over for you. But you simply dropped from sight."

"Actually Grace . . ."

"Oh, and look now, here comes that nice stewardess. What was her name?" The signaling hand rose again. Bunkie and Stash came toward the booth, looking serene after their night on the town.

"Teddie," said Bunkie, "didn't you get my message? We called to ask you to breakfast this morning. And here you are."

"Summoned by the Fates," I said.

"Everybody want coffee?" asked Grace.

"I'll have tea," said Stash.

The waitress looked annoyed at this defiance.

"Arrest her, Stash," said Bunkie, when the waitress had moved off.

"Ohhh. Are you a police officer, Miss Stash?" said Grace Bombadil as if she were about to feel safer by half.

"Yes ma'am," said Stash, looking uncomfortable. "In New Orleans."

"Such a colorful city," murmured Grace.

"Stash is a vice officer," said Bunkie, with a mischievous half-smile.

"Are you here on 'business?'" asked Grace, looking about her.

"I'd rather not say, ma'am, if you don't mind."

"Oh Stash," said Bunkie, expertly guiding the tea in her friend's direction, instead of in front of me where the waitress wanted to put it, "you do crave secrecy. I'm sure there's no harm in telling Mrs. Bombadil that you are here attending a convention."

"In *this* hotel? Why I had no idea that anything was going on beyond Tupperware. I'm sure Teddie here shares my surprise. Don't you dear?"

"Well, actually, I've been trying to explain that I'm not with Tupperware."

"You're not?" exclaimed Bunkie and Grace Bombadil in unison.

"Then you must be in vice," continued the older woman.

Bunkie and Stash looked at each other, then turned away, stifling a laugh.

"Modern languages," I said, pointing to my name tag.

She took a pair of jeweled half-glasses out of her

purse and set them on her nose, leaning forward. " 'Arden Benbow, English Department, UCLA.' Why my dear, I don't understand."

"Neither do I," I said, finishing my coffee. "But I have an appointment in ten minutes on the twenty-second floor."

When I got into the elevator I realized Grace Bombadil was right. Academics and vice officers were hard to tell apart. Everybody in the elevator looked as if they knew a secret they were not about to divulge. Also, everybody was male except for me and one other person. I looked at her. She looked at me.

It was Jane Oliver in that elevator.

"Jane?" I said.

"Arden?" she said.

The vice squad stiffened. Then the door opened on the twenty-second floor, and Jane and I stepped out together. The doors closed behind us. My limbic system began to tune up.

No, I told it. Today's concert has been canceled.

When we embraced, a single oboe sounded over a distant pond. I burst into tears.

She was holding my face in her hands when the elevator doors opened and a woman who looked like Professor Gridley got out.

"Come on, Oliver. The first candidate will be here any minute. Oh, is that you, Benbow?" She craned her head between us and read my name tag. "Michaels," she said. "Bertha Michaels. Assistant Chair." For a moment I thought my name had changed again. She put out her hand and demonstrated a firm handshake, confirming it was she who was Bertha Michaels. "Well, come along, then," she said.

She led the way down the corridor and flung a door open. Jane squeezed my hand quickly and then let go. There were four people sitting about on the bed and a chair or two. Then a short man with eyebrows like caterpillars rose — holding his head atilt so the caterpillars would not slide off — and motioned me to his seat. "Booth Hazard," he said, pressing a moist hand momentarily into mine. "Chair."

I did not know whether he referred to himself or to the furniture he had just relinquished. But I sat down.

"This is Miss Benbow from UCLA," said Bertha Michaels. "She comes highly recommended by my old friend Frances Gridley, who is of course known among Victorians of the highest water." When she smiled her lips rose a shade over her gums, making her look like a horse I once knew named Gin Rickey.

"Professor St. John, who heads our Creative Writing Program, no doubt will wish a word with you."

Everybody looked at a lanky man in his late forties who sprawled all over the pillow part of a single bed. He was gazing fixedly out the window behind me. When he finally did say something I gave a little leap of surprise inside myself.

"Tell me Miss Benbow, can poetry be taught?"

It sounded like a rhetorical question, so I waited politely.

"Well, can it!"

"It seems to me —"

"Of course it can't! Anybody tell you differently is a damned liar and a humbug."

"What Professor St. John means," began a

soft-spoken young woman trying to stay upright on the bed next to him, "is that while the teaching of creative writ—"

"I'll be damned if I need you as my interpreter, Paige."

"We are very proud of our writing program," said The Chair in a firm, clear voice. "It has a growing national reputation."

"Reputation, me backsides," murmured St. John, readjusting himself on the bed and returning his gaze to the window.

"Miss Paige, here —" Professor Hazard nodded in the direction of the soft-spoken young woman, "— has, for example, won a grant from the American Poetic Society that will allow her to take a year's leave."

Miss Paige blushed.

"May I ask, Benbow, about your plans for publication?" whinnied Professor Michaels.

I pulled the lawyer's empty briefcase onto my lap out of sheer nervousness, but it must have seemed a subtle and wise gesture.

"Ah, she knows. She knows. That's a smart one," said St. John, seized with a sudden interest. " 'Publication is the auction of the human mind' was how Emily Dickinson put it and she was by God right. Let's hire this woman."

Had he mistaken me for Emily Dickinson? I am always stimulated by the insane. "Yes," I found myself saying, "and Virginia Woolf said, 'Poetry is a voice answering a voice.' "

"*Orlando!*" called Jane Oliver from the back of the room, her voice striking my heart like sun through stained glass.

CHAPTER 12:
Touching Down

Airplanes are fine places for gaining perspective. Just as land and towns and even swimming pools get turned into little decorative squares of the human quilt, so too is overwhelming experience rendered down into squares of fabric, a part of the great quilt the goddess is stitching together. I had looked forward to my return flight for this reason, even though my epiphany would have to manifest itself within forty minutes' flight time.

I settled back into my window seat, stuffing the tiny airline pillow under my head, and began deep breathing, prelude to enlightenment.

Once I had started the deep breathing, something strange began to happen. I could not stop the deep breathing. When I tried, I gulped. The lady next to me was beginning to stare. This breathing was decidedly not meditation. This breathing was fear.

I had never read *Fear of Flying* for fear it would make me fear flying. And now I had arrived at that terrible state on my own.

With awesome clarity I felt the plane falling away beneath me, saw baggage and umbrellas flying, heard babies screaming, was struck on the head with the descending oxygen mask, witnessed people with terminal diseases throwing themselves over others to protect them from impact. And then — silence.

Nothing. There might eventually be a small sound within the wreckage lodged in that remote, windswept Tibetan mountaintop. A hostess crawling out of the pantry, perhaps. But I would not hear. Arden Benbow would be no more.

When I looked up from my corpse, the maintenance crew was removing trash and lost belongings from empty seats.

Topaz and I stood watching the baggage carrousel revolve. Only an army duffel bag, a black cardboard suitcase, and a tennis racket remained. Ruth's blue Samsonite luggage was once more off seeking its fortune.

"The black cardboard suitcase," I said, "belongs to a paroled murderer."

"Who has abducted," he replied, "the lady colonel and the tennis pro."

"All of whom must now outfit themselves out of Ruth's strange suitcase."

"They'll be picked up crossing the border at Piedras Negras."

"What if, Topaz, life is one big baggage carrousel?"

"Come on," said Topaz, "we'll report the suitcase and get the hell out of here."

Topaz had parked outside at the curb. "Driving a hearse has its advantages," he said, handing me my cane and slamming the car door. "But not many." He opened his own door, carefully picking up his pith helmet and sunglasses before sitting down. "Mixed media," he explained, putting on the hat and glasses, then checking himself and the traffic in the rearview mirror.

We edged out into the mayhem. "We could paint it," I said. "Something festive. Sky blue, perhaps."

"I'm glad you're back," he said, throwing his big arm around my shoulders.

"It feels like six years," I said. "How's everybody?"

"Kip bought a skateboard with the money he earned typing your job letters. He is also growing a beard. Hillary has been invited to a New Year's Eve party and says she doesn't want to go with Chuck. It's not a very promising name but I gave her the standard lecture on appearance and reality. She's mulling it over. The dog threw up on your bedroom rug. Arthur dropped his cornet out a second-story window and says it doesn't sound right. I never thought it did, but far be it from me to impede the arts. Alice has some news she wants to give you herself but will be late tonight on account of work. I can tell you though that Ruth's day at the beauty parlor was not an unmitigated success."

"No?"

"The cut was okay, a big improvement actually. But she went swimming in the company pool and her hair turned green."

"Green?" I said.

We snorted.

"Green? Really?"

"Green."

"Kind of a lime color?"

"The very same."

We snorted again.

"Alice would say we're being cruel."

"Yes," he yelped. "She would." And we laughed till we cried.

I flipped out the overhead light in the girls' room, but Jamie's reading light still illuminated her page and her chin.

"What're you reading?" I asked, kneeling down and resting my head on a supine Raggedy Ann.

"*Jane Eyre,*" she said. "Last night I read the part where Mr. Rochester asks Jane to marry him even though he already has a wife locked up in his attic."

"And what would you do if you were Jane?"

"I wouldn't marry Mr. Rochester," she said. "He might lock me up too. No, I'd do what she did."

"And what was that?" I asked, placing my rough hand on her soft one. "I don't remember."

"Well, the moon comes in at her window that night and tells her to flee. And Jane says, "Mother, I will." Then she just throws on her clothes and follows the road out of there. I'm reading it again tonight. It makes me cry when she calls the moon 'mother.' "

"Me too," I said, snuffling. "Isn't it wonderful." She squeezed my arm and I tiptoed out.

Alice was waiting for me on the porch. I grabbed my jacket from the peg by the door and went outside. It felt good to wear my own clothes again, and to be going to meet my Alice in a way that was as soft and familiar as this old jacket. I could see her silhouette in the wicker chair, her empress chair. When she sat there, all the power that belonged by rights to her seemed to collect from wherever the day had scattered it and settle upon her like the peace of evening. I bent and kissed her soft mouth.

"Arden," she said, grabbing my hand. "Sit down. There's something I need to tell you."

I pulled my chair up close and held both her hands as if I could ground the current that was about to leap through my veins.

"I've been offered a vice-presidency."

"But that's wonderf— Oh," I said, pulling up.

"Yes," she said. "It is, and it's not."

"But what will we do?" I asked, looking out at the barn, the milling rabbits, the fence, and the Jane Eyre moon beyond.

CHAPTER 13:
Long Distance

Since my mother's astute Tarot reading last month, every time I saw her my mind was seized with a montage of people falling out of towers, hanging by one foot, being trampled by wild horses, or impaled by swords. Here we were on New Year's Eve, sitting together on the decaying couch while Alice, Topaz, Ruth, and other revelers hung crepe paper and blew up balloons.

I was already in what I think of as my Baggie

Mood even before my mother arrived early to help. The Baggie Mood is when you feel so far removed from people and events around you that you become an observer rather than a participant. Others seem reduced in size and incapable of projecting their tiny voices loud enough that you can hear them. Sound reaches you — if at all — as if from great distances, like light from a dead planet. You are inside your warm and moist Ziploc.

Against this backdrop, my mother pushed her cup of eggnog in the general direction of my heart and said, in reference to the near future, "It doesn't look all that good. I'm not going to lie to you." She bent her Clairol blonde head and looked at me, all in the same gesture. When she does that she looks a lot like an Afghan hound I used to know named Raquel.

"I'm just a Fatima," I said cheerlessly.

"Well, what're you going to do? You can't raise six children by yourself."

"I've done it before," I said, gulping eggnog and hoping it would glide into my stomach and supply a soft cushion later for food or grief.

She leaned back into the deep couch cushions and stared at the ceiling.

"Cal State Fresno is interested. At least I could come home for weekends."

"Fresno is where they make movies about people whose lives are falling apart. James Dean died there."

"In an agricultural setting."

"We are not agricultural people, Arden."

"Your parents were," I reminded.

"The King of Spain gave my grandparents real estate."

"And what did they do with it?"

"Sold it, of course. They were not ignorant, whatever you may think."

"I think I'll get some eggnog," I said rising.

"And you'd better answer that telephone too," she said.

"What telephone?" I asked from my Baggie.

The truth is, I hate telephones. If I have to have one I prefer to store it in a closed drawer. I'd rather walk three miles and deliver my message in person than lift a receiver. I read a novel once where one of the characters said it this way: "The telephone is a modern symbol for communications which will never take place." Exactly. And anyone at all can come over that line and threaten your life or your sanity. Remember Joan Crawford in *Dial M for Murder?* Well, every time the phone rings, I feel just like Joan Crawford.

By the time I had made my way through the merry-makers and into the bedroom I was in a state. "Hello," I growled.

"Arden," said a voice like a cello bowing a minor chord. "Is that you?"

What could I say, "Let's assume it is?" I laughed, then bit my lip with vexation.

"Arden, the reason I'm calling is . . ."

"Jane, you don't have to have a reason," I found myself saying.

"But the reason is Professor Hazard is going to make you an offer tonight."

"An offer?"

"St. John likes you. He didn't like anybody else we interviewed."

"I hardly opened my mouth."

"Anyway," she said, "I wanted you to know

before Professor Hazard calls. And to wish you a Happy New Year." She drew her bow across her strings once or twice more and was gone.

I stared at the receiver. Maybe I should revise my feelings about the telephone. It obviously was here to stay. I set it gently into its princess cradle, admiring the faint glow around the finger holes.

But it rang again. It might be Barbara Stanwyck's murderer. Or The Chair with his offer.

Worse yet, it was Gridley.

"You're phone's been tied up all evening," she said by way of greeting. "Has Booth got through yet?"

"Booth?"

"The Chair at Midway."

Not furniture, I reminded myself.

"My old friend Bertha Michaels — Assistant Chair, you may recall — says Booth will call some time tonight. They're anxious to get things settled, and it seems you've really impressed their poet, St. John."

I smiled.

"Benbow, are you there?"

"Ma'am," I said.

"Well, there's a certain naivete about you — not without its charm, I hasten to add — that may impede these negotiations. To be brief, Benbow, I have some advice for you.

"One, remember you have six children. You'll need a decent salary. You're going to have to bargain for it. They won't just give it to you, though their endowments have always been generous. Partly you want to show them you're savvy by driving them to the wall.

"Two, the job market is depressed right now. Midway is certainly not the best small college in the world but it's not the worst. The quality of their students leaves something to be desired, but children from wealthy families are entitled to an education too. I hope we have not come to the point where education is a perquisite of the poor."

Here she gave that little hamster laugh and I knew I did not want to go to Midway College.

"Three, do not be dissuaded by the location of the college. Some of our finest scholars have come out of the South. And some of our finest writers too.

"In short, Benbow, it would be sign of frivolity and ingratitude if you did not take this job I have worked so hard to secure for you."

I felt a parody of her hamster sound rising like a growl from deep in my throat. But she would take it as mere satire and not the death-threat I intended. So I closed my teeth and emitted an ambiguous tone.

"Good," she said, and hung up.

I threw the phone against one wall and my primal scream against another.

"Mom?" said Jamie, sticking her head through the door.

"Just rage," I said, falling back on the bed.

I heard her New Year's pumps crossing hardwood then carpet, heard her resettling the phone on the nightstand. I lifted an eyelid.

"Somebody might want to call," she explained.

"Doubtless," I said.

The phone rang. We looked at each other.

* * * * *

Back in the living room Guy Lombardo was playing and the crepe paper ceiling decoration had relaxed its grasp on the hundred balloons. My uncles were playing poker on the dining room table, my mother sat on the sagging couch, Max asleep on one knee, Ellen on the other, and Shelden sloping against her right shoulder. Two couples danced in the dim light.

"May I cut in?" I asked Tom. He was wearing diapers. Topaz was dressed as Father Time.

"Yes, but he doesn't like it if you try to lead."

"I'm not in the mood to lead," I said.

"Sounds serious," said Topaz, tucking my head under his fatherly beard and somehow relieving me of one hundred pounds of my dead weight. We waltzed around the couch, avoiding my mother's Red Cross shoes.

"I've been offered a job," I whispered.

"That's wonderful."

"Not really," I said. "It's that strange school in Florida where all the writing faculty are named after spices. Rosemary, Sage, Coriander, Cumin."

"What're they paying? Strange has its own appeal, if the price is right."

"I don't want to live in Florida."

"Why not? You got sun there. You got your beaches and your ocean."

"I don't want to live in the South."

"Florida's not the South. Florida's just Florida. They make orange juice and nobody's got to wear ties. Don't you ever go to the movies?"

"My father left Texas in a box car. That should tell me something."

"Texas," said Topaz, pausing and holding me at arm's length. "Texas is another story. Texas is where they lynch you for looking at a white woman. Or a white man either, for that matter. You won't catch me in no Texas."

"Maybe I should have accepted," I mused.

"You turned them down? That only leaves the Permian Basin and Fresno. The Permian Basin is in Texas. Your dead father tells you no. Besides, remember they told you the Permian Basin wasn't a city, it was a geological formation? Who wants to live on a geological formation? Geological formations got no culture. And Fresno. Do you think Fresno has ballet? That leaves Florida. Call them back and say we'll come."

He twirled me around as if for punctuation and dipped me slowly back, from which vantage point I could see Alice patiently teaching Ruth to dance.

At that moment backward counting began in the kitchen and spread to the living room, the chanting of numbers falling in with the beat of my heart and the release of a hundred balloons. I went to make a phone call.

CHAPTER 14:
Tamales

"Florida's a good place to go if you have to go someplace," said my mother, dropping a tear into the bowl of masa and stirring well. "I could visit you there. It's warm and has Disneyworld."

"What do you put in the meat?" I asked, leaning over a pot on the counter. "I'll have to learn to do this myself."

"Oh, it's just machaca," she said with a wave of her hand. "You can use turkey instead. Or pork."

I picked up a damp corn husk. "It's a good job," I said. "They pay well."

"It's time you made a little money, Arden." She took the corn husk out of my hand and spread masa on it with the back of a spoon. "Now put in the machaca and a couple of grapes."

"Grapes?"

"Your grandmother always used grapes. Makes them special. That was her secret. Nobody ever knew what it was. Just the family."

I set two grapes on top of the machaca. She took the laden corn husk out of my hand, rolling it quickly, and tying thread around one end.

"You've got to let me do this, you know. Or I'll never learn."

"You move so slowly," she said. "You always have."

"I like detail," I said. "I like to meditate over what I'm doing." I took the tamale out of her hand and began wrapping thread around its opposite end. "I like the feel and look of things. The smell of them." I tied my knot, then took the tamale into my hand, holding it close to my mother's bifocals. "This tamale is the same as a poem," I explained.

"Arden, sometimes I worry about you. What if Shelden is right and you *are* crazy? I mean, it's a possibility. And you going off to Florida where we can't help you." She took the tamale out of my hand and set it into the steamer. "All those children and no Alice."

I picked up another corn husk. "Use the spoon," she said. "You always spread masa with the back of a spoon."

"Remember," I said, gesturing with a corn husk,

"at Nona's house the day before Thanksgiving when all the aunts would come over and line up along one wall and turn out tamales like they were on an assembly line."

"And talk," she said, holding a grape poised. "The stories they told."

"I could only pick out a word here and there —"

"And going a mile a minute —"

"Words and fingers flying —"

"Until the last tamale."

My mother sighed and wiped her hands. "That's how to make tamales. And Shelden needs a hundred of these for his business meeting tonight. I wish my mother were here now, and her five sisters."

"I will try," I said, kissing the smudge of masa on her cheek, "to shape these tamales with both the swiftness of my grandmother and the intensity of a poet."

CHAPTER 15:
Members of the Cast

I swung open the door of my blue hearse. We were nearing the Ides of March and the time seemed unpropitious for removing my cast. My mother had called last night saying my horoscope warned against handling machinery.

After all, I thought, reaching for Aunt Vi's cane, the prohibition was against me and not against Dr. Caswell.

The office was dim after the afternoon sunlight. I nodded in the direction of the blue-rimmed eyeglasses behind the receptionist's window and took a chair opposite an immense woman in a body cast. Tight little curls like link sausages covered her head. A copy of *Woman's Day* balanced on one knee, she peered over her cheekbones in the direction of the page far below.

Then her eyes wandered to my cast, where the print proved even more difficult to read. "Yours itch?" she asked confidentially. "I like to died last night. Couldn't get to sleep for the life of me till Harry, he reaches in with this teen-ninesy Roto-Rooter some salesman sold him from plumbers' supply. Never been worth a lick, he says, as a proper tool. But I tell you it give me some relief." She rolled her eyes back in a bliss of recollection, then flicked them open suddenly, like a giant doll. "Say, you a Leo? You got a nose like a Leo."

I smiled. "Aquarian."

"Watch out for machinery then. And don't start any new projects."

"I wouldn't dream of it," I said.

A horn sounded from the parking lot. "That'd be Harry," she said, as if introducing him. Then she began a strange little rocking motion, as if in time to distant music.

"Need some help?" I asked.

She nodded, building momentum, then rocked herself up and into my arms. We struggled for balance momentarily, then caught it, with the grace of the Flying Wallendas.

"Now," she said, squeezing my elbow and bending

her tight little curls so close they tickled my ear, "that Saturn that's been worrying you — what's it been, nearly two years now? — is fixing to be gone."

The front door closed behind her just as the nurse called my name. I followed the smell of Niagara starch down a corridor, listening for the last time to the curious rhythm of shoe, cane, and cast against linoleum. "What walks on three feet in the evening?" I said, looking at my shoe.

"I beg your pardon?" said the nurse brightly.

"I said, 'One can get used to anything.' "

"Well," she said in the tone of one used to dealing with other people's clinical depressions, "it will feel good to get that nasty old cast off."

She left me perched on the examining table, with nothing to read but the walls and hardware. On one wall was a colorful, shiny poster of an anatomically correct male. It was hard to relate to. I had better luck with skeletons, though Dr. Caswell's was only a graphic reproduction and could not hold a candle to the real one in Dr. Escobar's waiting room.

Certainly we carried a lot of bones around with us. I pulled my pant leg above my cast and tried to see with Superman eyes. What if all the muscle had disappeared, leaving nothing but bone as thin as skim milk? In Mexico they buried nuns and dug them up again to see if their fingernails and hair had grown, to see if they had died in despair. Those who passed the test they canonized, encasing in glass a section of bone, an arm or leg. Bones to worship. I saw my leg bones enclosed in glass and put on display outside the English Reading Room, saw Professor Gridley staring with scholarly interest, taking notes on three by five cards, then passing on.

The door opened. Dr. Caswell wanted to know how we were today.

"Listen, Doctor, you're not an Aquarian, are you?"

He gave the smile reserved for lunatics. "A Virgo, matter of fact."

He picked up an implement that looked like an electric pizza cutter. Its blade began to whir and grow invisible.

Virgos are careful people. Their houses are neat and clean. They work hard and well at whatever they do. This one applied his pizza cutter to the top of my cast and slowly ran it down my tibia, southward toward my toes.

How does the snake feel when it sheds its skin? Listen, metamorphosis costs extra.

At last Dr. Caswell silenced his engine of liberation, dug his thumbs into either side of the cast, and cracked it open like an egg.

CHAPTER 16:
Lunch with Valentine

I sat at Professor Gridley's picnic table and watched her toss hot dogs onto her brand new red grill. The hot dogs were the kind encased with paper that must be peeled off before cooking. Gridley had not peeled them. I sipped cheap champagne out of my Dixie cup and smiled to myself. Little lines of fire started along some of the dogs. Gridley, wearing an immaculate barbecue apron bearing the words KISS THE COOK, looked benignly at the group of graduate students she had gathered in honor of those under her tutelage who had somehow survived their doctoral defenses. Graciously she had included me in the group, notwithstanding my defection to the Creative Writing Program late in my lamentable career. Still, I had successfully defended my dissertation and Professor Greenlock, my major professor, had told my committee afterward that my collection of poems would be a hot contender for the Starmont Poetry Award. Gridley liked to place herself along any longitudinal lines where praise might pass.

Puffs of black smoke began to rise from the hot dogs, and Gridley called cheerily, "Bring your plates, everybody." A dark-eyed young man in Criticism leaped to the head of the line. Everybody knew him as the Savage because he always crouched in his seminar chair, feet on the seat, head bobbing up and down in expressions of wonder and contempt. He grabbed three or four hot dogs with his hands, slung several buns on top, and made for the picnic table. I quickly rose and got in line behind Cup Cake, who carried Ding Dongs in his important-looking briefcase, and Smiling Realism, who always looked on the brighter side while keeping one eye on the main chance.

I did not want to sit next to the Savage, who crouched on his heels feeding at the picnic table, or Cup Cake, who would want to talk about the structure of reality. Smiling Realism was beginning to croon over Gridley's silver relish tray, her kindness, her house, her accomplishments. The line behind her was growing. I moved off, selecting a yellow canvas chair under a yellow umbrella where I could watch safely.

A door opened and a tall, elderly woman stepped onto the patio. She wore her smooth gray hair ear-length; it curved gently toward her jaw line. She paused, glancing in the direction of the barbecue and the collection of people. Gridley looked up, giving a little gesture the other woman immediately understood as an invitation but which she declined. Instead, lifting her champagne glass in salute, she moved on in my direction.

She settled herself in the chair next to mine. "I wanted to match, you see." She indicated her yellow pants and smiled, then extended her hand. "I'm Ada. An inmate, I'm afraid."

"Arden Benbow," I said, taking her cool hand.

"Yes, I know. Val talks about you all the time."

"Val?"

"Your Dr. Gridley. Valentine Gridley, but don't tell her I told you."

It had certainly never occurred to me that Gridley had a first name, much less a lover. I had seen her at university functions with a pipe-chuffing professor of history whom we referred to as the Stuffed Moose. But a lover. Impossible. "Valentine," I said out loud.

"Valentine. Her mother was much taken with Valentino, it seems."

I picked up my hot dog absently and took a bite. The scorched paper crackled against my teeth.

"Cooking is not Val's forte. I hope you won't choke to death out of politeness."

I withdrew my teeth just in time. The Savage had gone back for seconds, while Smiling Realism sat next to Gridley trying to remember all her mother had ever said about discreetly disposing of culinary disasters. In little clusters of chairs beneath eucalyptus trees, former graduate students pulled paper from their teeth and orthodontia, glancing nervously in Gridley's direction.

"Oh, my," said Ada, stifling a laugh. "I think I'd better bring the dessert."

"Shall I help?"

"Please, dear."

I followed her across the grass and then the dappled patio, where bougainvillaea-covered lattice made possible this paradox of sun and shade. The kitchen was cool and dim. On the table rested three large white plates covered with bright petit fours.

"More champagne?" she offered. "The good stuff's in here." Instead of reaching into an ice-filled washtub she opened the refrigerator and brought out something expensive. Then she took my Dixie cup and cast it into the trash, retrieving from an upper cabinet a champagne glass the twin of hers. "I'm so very glad to meet you at last."

"I'm so glad to know you exist."

"But didn't you suspect?"

"Not really," I said. "Alice claims always to *know*, but my radar's not very finely tuned I sometimes think."

"Well, certainly Val is supremely 'careful,' as she puts it. Perhaps more than she needs to be. But she says history is cyclical, that if she relaxed her vigil, around it would come again and she'd be caught. And who knows? Maybe she's right. She and I have certainly lived through some hard times."

"How long have you been together?"

"Oh, eons," she laughed. "Nearly thirty years."

"That's wonderful."

"Yes, I count it among the Seven Wonders

153

myself." She gazed through the kitchen window. "When will you be leaving?" she asked, turning.

"I was just thinking about that. Soon. May, probably. I'll need to teach summer school. Alice isn't coming with me. At least not for a while."

"I'm sorry," said Ada. "I'm very sorry for that."

"So am I," I said, my eyes suddenly filling.

She took me in her arms with a great lightness, not as if assuming my pain but rather dispelling it. I rested on her mother-warmth, breathing in her cleanness and a touch of White Linen.

CHAPTER 17:
Garage Sale

When spring comes to Los Angeles, people do not fall in love, they have garage sales.

Objects are spread out on card tables, picnic tables, coffee tables; mementos labeled, priced, and assorted into baskets, boxes, jars, and bags — the visible emblems of the contents of a person's life, before which the curious will eventually assemble.

To have a garage sale takes a certain courage, not only a certain willingness to risk by displaying these intimate tokens, these artifacts of a private life, but also a willingness to part with them, to say, "I am something more than the sum total of my accumulated goods."

Maybe I should have just fallen in love.

Anyway, picture early April, a foggy Saturday morning, about six. The house is wrapped in the kind of silence fog brings, where sounds seem far away and can be absorbed easily into our dreams. Swathed in terry cloth I move through the rooms and the dreams of my sleepers toward coffee. Polly Perk emits subdued chuffs from the kitchen. I go to the front window, lean on the sill, studying the gray air and trees.

Something moves. Beside the road, inside an ancient Studebaker the color of fog, hunches a bargain-hunter. I know him. He buys what is broken, incomplete, unrealized. Especially appliances. Thirty-seven Waring blenders, nineteen toasters with frayed cords, a dozen scorched waffle irons. He has come to the right place. But two hours early.

I sigh and wander into the kitchen. Vaguely I feel that vultures have come to roost. I pour my coffee, move to the back door, and stare through the screen into the carport, stage for the impending garage sale drama.

Hanging from an extension ladder are a dozen ties I never wear and my mauve suspenders. The mauve suspenders I have second thoughts about, but I renew hastily my vow to travel light. Then there is the card table covered with Hillary's cast-off costume jewelry, my collection of World War II medals given to me by my uncles, a tenor saxophone on which I never progressed past "The Sheik of Araby," and my fishing boots. Next to that is a large collection of baby gear, from satin booties — nearly new — to a cradle my Uncle Ukie made with his pocket knife. I notice that on the washing machine, surrounded by broken small appliances, Arthur has casually placed his cornet, as if by accident. Near the garage door, my Harley Davidson is resting on its kick-stand, the side car disconnected.

I brush past a forest of discarded clothes, pausing briefly to sweep my uncles' medals into the pocket of my robe, then make my way to my motorcycle, rest my hand on the saddle. Why not, says my Indian self, opening the garage door. I kick-start the engine, feeling a faint twinge along the faultline of my leg, then settle into the saddle, my robe and pajamas tucked close around me. Then down the drive I roar and past the drawn-up cars of early hunters.

CHAPTER 18:
Who's On First?

I had a strange sense of misgiving as I opened the hearse's back door for my two daughters. "Listen," I said, sliding in next to Hillary, "I don't understand why weddings require rehearsals. We didn't have a rehearsal, did we, Alice?"

"No dear," said Alice, placing her right arm on the back of the driver's seat and deftly backing out.

"That's because," said Topaz, "you were acting

from the heart. It's only art that requires rehearsals. Take it from one who knows."

"It's a tradition," said Alice, shifting into Drive and leaping into the evening traffic.

"What's tradition?" asked Hillary, who is ten.

"With any kind of luck, you will never know," I said, sinking into the black plush seat that still smelled of flowers and embalming fluid.

"On the plus side of tradition, though," said Topaz, turning to look at Hillary, "without tradition we would not be riding in this fine automobile, and without tradition you would not be going out into this fair evening to practice being a ring bearer and to eat a wonderful and free meal at a proper restaurant."

"Sounds okay to me," said my practical Hil.

"I'd rather be home reading," said Jamie ruefully. "How many times is Daddy going to get married, anyway?"

"Beats me, honey," said Topaz.

"I like Monica," said Hillary. "I don't care how many times he gets married. He'll still be our father."

"Of course he will," said Alice. "None of that ever changes."

"I like having lots of mothers," said Hillary. "There's Alice and Frances and Monica and Topaz . . ."

"And Mom," said Jamie.

"Of course Mom. She's the Mom of Moms."

I gave her a hug and a kiss as Alice turned into the church parking lot.

Uke the Duke was just getting out of his truck

two cars down. He jingled toward us wearing his suit and cowboy boots.

"Jesus," he said, after kissing his great-nieces and everybody else, "I never been a best man before."

"I'm just an usher," said Topaz. "I wanted to be maid of honor."

"Silly," said Hillary. "Alice is maid of honor."

"Only because Dad didn't want Mom to be," said Jamie.

"That's fine," I told her. "I'd really rather watch."

"Me too," said Jamie, "more than anything."

"Let's go inside," said Alice.

We followed the maid of honor.

Inside it was a little dim. Religion seems to require faint lighting. We paused. Malthus spotted us and steamed in our direction.

"Thank heaven you're here," he said, apparently influenced by the religious atmosphere. "Lord help us, Monica's mother can't make the rehearsal. She and the aunt are grounded in Dallas. Bad weather. Arden, you'll have to stand in for her. We need you to give Monica away."

"To give Monica away?"

"Yes, I just explained all that." He nipped his breath in the way he does when dealing with necessary lunatics.

"Daddies give brides away," said Hillary, who was revealing an alarming aptitude for tradition.

"Monica's daddy couldn't come, sweetheart. Besides —" Malthus paused, looking as if something had caught sideways in his throat, "— Monica wanted her mother to give her away."

It was clear there had been a few friendly

discussions about tradition in *this* family, as well as our own. Malthus by now had a firm grasp on my arm and was propelling me in the direction of a red-faced clergyman.

"This woman will give Monica away," Malthus announced. Monica looked at me oddly.

"Fine, fine," said Christ's representative, pumping my hand absently and staring about the room. "Now places everybody. Ushers, you can sit down. Monica you can sit down too. The bride never rehearses, you know. We'll get you a stand-in."

"Alice," said Malthus. "Alice can do that."

"I'm the maid of honor," said Alice.

"Well . . . that doesn't matter," said Malthus, with a wave of his hand. "Just pretend you're standing next to yourself."

"I don't understand," said Hillary.

"Hillary, you enter just before the bride and her father. I mean mother."

"But who are the bride and mother? I can't remember."

Apparently her father couldn't remember either. He stood still, slowly raising his hand to his bald spot.

"Here now," said the good reverend, elbowing his way into the center of discussion, "Alice, I believe. Alice is the bride and she enters on the arm of . . ."

"My wife," said Malthus in his confusion.

"Your wife!" said the reverend.

"I mean Arden here," he recovered.

"Yes, quite so," said the reverend, taking a white handkerchief out of his back pocket and mopping his brow. "First come the bridesmaids. That's it." He pulled the reluctant Jamie by her wrist, and Hillary fell in behind her. "Next comes the mother on the arm of . . . but no." Red crept up what you could see of the reverend's throat. "The mother is giving the bride . . . well then next we need the ring bearer. Where is the little chap?"

"Here I am," said Hillary.

"Ah . . . quite so. And behind this little lady we have, of course, the bride on the arm of her father. I mean her mother. Mrs. Benbow, that would be. Well now, everybody line up behind me and when I move out, please, everybody walk like this."

We would try. I took Alice's arm and we queued up behind our daughters. At the signal we began mincing forward, not to the strains of triumphal music, but to the reverend's "And one and two and one and two." When I looked up, we were moving toward Malthus, as sure as Fate.

In pantomime I was turning Alice, the love of my life, over to Malthus, while on the level of flat-out reality, tomorrow afternoon I would be allowing the innocent Monica James to wander straight into the clutches of Malthus. Was I free only with the proviso that I find a replacement?

But wait a minute, I thought, I am not Monica's mother. Or even her father, for that matter. Either Monica was giving herself away, or her flesh-and-blood mother, now snoozing gently in an airport terminal two thousand miles away, would tomorrow perform that service with no help from me. I breathed again.

Two hours later we all congregated at the restaurant across the street for the ritual known as Rehearsal Dinner. I stared into my cold consommé. On a sea of brown grease floated a transparent lemon slice and a dead spring of parsley. Generosity was alien to Malthus. He might never marry again in his whole life, if three proved to be the charm people say it is, but he had selected the cheapest dinner for his guests that the Thistle Inn would still call its own. Malthus was so cheap he washed out Baggies and hung them on a tiny clothesline over the sink.

Did Monica know the appalling facts of Malthus' household economies? I looked up to see her steering a straight course in my direction through the milling rehearsal party. She picked up the place card next to mine, substituted her own, and sat down.

"That was very strange," she said, pale and breathless.

"Which part?" I asked.

"The part where you gave Alice away to Malthus, only it was me you were giving."

"I know," I said, returning my eyes to the torpid consommé. "But I wasn't me then, I was your mother, as I recall."

"Is there something you ought to tell me?"

"I've often wondered," I said, looking at last into her blue eyes.

"Monica!" said Malthus, steaming up from my blind side. "Dear, you're sitting in the wrong place. We're at the head of the table. Remember?"

"I need to talk to Arden," she said very distinctly.

"To Arden!" He leaned close to his Intended, tried for a whisper, but said audibly, "And just how in hell do you think that makes me look, you sitting next to my goddamned wife?"

"I am not your wife," I gently reminded him.

"I know that, for chrissakes. What kind of idiot do you take me for?"

I smiled.

"We'll talk about this later," he said to Monica, tightening his fingers momentarily around her upper arm, then stalking back to the head of the table.

"What's going on?" asked Alice, leaning close.

"Gnats in paradise," I said, lifting the spent parsley from my soup and holding it dripping between my thumb and forefinger.

CHAPTER 19:
Absolution

"Dear," I said the following night, sliding my foot across the bed to touch Alice's leg, "do you think it's my fault Monica's not getting married to Malthus?"

"It may be to your credit, but certainly not your fault." She plumped up her pillow and held her arm out, inviting a snuggle, the way she does when she thinks I'm being too Catholic.

"Are you going to be all right?" I asked.

"I think so."

"I'm not sure why we're doing this," I said. "Did I know once?"

"It comes and goes."

"We're not doing it simply because we've started, are we?"

"No," said Alice, "I think it's something more than that. Don't you?"

"Are we growing again?" I asked.

"Maybe," she said.

"My joints ache so," I said. "Hold me."

CHAPTER 20:
Maps

"What's that banging sound?" I said, looking up from the map spread out on the dining room table.

"Beats the hell out of me," said Topaz, rubbing his eyes and setting aside his pink marker.

"Shall I take a look?" asked Tom, rising from his chair and stretching.

Alice streaked past and out the front door, followed by Arthur in his pajamas, then the dog.

"They're in the U-Haul and won't come out," said

Jamie, hanging briefly in the hall doorway. "Maybe you need to talk to them again."

"Ah," said Tom. "Separation anxiety. I've got some of that myself."

"Do they dress like *Gone With the Wind* where we're going?" asked Hillary, coming in from the kitchen with two dishtowels stuffed into the top of her dress.

"Hil, it's time for bed," I said. "I'll call you as soon as I get there and give you a fashion update. Jamie, whose night is it for final roundup?" I leaned out the screen door as Max and Ellen leaped out of the trailer like paratroopers, then bounded toward me and the front door.

"Kip's got roundup," said Hillary, deflating her bosom for the evening. "But he's shaving again. It leaves little brown dots in the sink. Yuck."

"Maybe Mom can find us a house with two bathrooms," said Jamie.

"Top priority," I said. "What else?"

"My own room," said Kip, appearing in a shaving cream moustache.

"I don't want to be alone," said Ellen. "I can't sleep without Hil and Jamie. Is Bruce coming? Are the rabbits coming? How can Daddy find us?"

"Who knows the answers to Ellen's questions?" I asked, lifting her onto my lap.

"I do," said Max, looking serious.

"Good," I said. "Everybody get to bed except Max and Ellen. Reading privileges for Kip and Jamie. We'll be in for kisses in a minute."

Alice joined us at the table. She looked tired and her cheeks were flushed. I took her hand.

"Now Max," said Topaz. "Tell Private Ellen here what you know about Operation Southbound."

"Well," said Max, "tomorrow you and Mom go to Florida and find us a big house."

"I know that, silly," said Ellen.

"We stay here with Alice and sometimes Daddy till you find that house. Then we get on the airplane, but not Alice. Bruce rides in the back with the suitcases. Dog's can't sit in the seats."

"And the rabbits," added Ellen.

"No," said Max.

"The rabbits stay with me, dear," put in Alice softly.

"What about my bed and my toys and my books?" said Ellen.

"Some of our stuff goes with Mom in the U-Haul, some the truck will bring later," said Max. "Can I go to bed now?"

"Let me escort you, sir," said Topaz, rising and slinging Max up onto his back.

"Tom," said Ellen, "are you staying with us while Mom and Topaz drive to Florida?"

"I'll come and see you so often you'll get tired of me."

"Remember, duck, Topaz has to come back after we're settled and live with Tom."

"But we'll both come and visit you whenever we get a vacation," said Tom.

"How will you know where I live?" asked Ellen.

"Look, dear," I said, turning the map to face her, "this is the freeway right near us. See that big number ten? Now, tomorrow Topaz and I will get on right here and stay on this same highway until we get to this big ten over here. Right by the university." I put her finger on the blue X. "This is exactly where we'll live, Midway, Florida."

"Better write that down for me on a piece of paper," she said.

Tom handed me the tablet. I wrote the name of the town I'd never seen, then gave it to El. She wrote the name again on another sheet in careful kindergarten letters and handed it to me. "So you don't forget," she said, sliding down from my lap and loping for the bathroom.

BOOK III

CHAPTER 21:
Wing Dance

On the morning of my departure, while my family moved in muffled tones about my apparently sleeping body, my mind directed the movie of departure day. My model was *Flying Down to Rio,* a Fred Astaire movie short on plot and long on dancing. In the finale, three or four biplanes circle an elegant hotel on opening night. On each brilliantly lit wing a dozen sequined beauties, holding onto almost invisible tethers, tap dance out the mythic code of journey, discovery, the creation of a personal significance. Could it not be — I thought, mashing my pillow over my head and winding myself further into my striped sheet — that these tap dancers balanced precariously on airplane wings were the essence of identity itself? Were we not the sum total of all the tap dancers perched on the biplane of self?

I sat up in bed listening. The dog clicked past the bedroom door. "Bruce," I said, "are they all gone now?" Bruce backtracked and stared at me quizzically from the door.

I think of Bruce as the fourth mother. His lineage is as multifaceted as my own, though he looks more like a golden retriever than anything. When you ask him a question he does not understand, he barks. I had and he did.

Topaz gave an answering bark from the living room, then added, "And you better get your sweet ass in gear. We got a world to do before lift off."

"I was thinking of Fred Astaire," I said, sliding off the bed in my sheet and tottering into the living room.

Topaz was standing next to a pile of boxes, a clipboard in his hand. "Big Jim's out back," he said, "thinning the herd." Big Jim raises Old English Sheepdogs in Topanga Canyon and tends to fix our plumbing. It was Big Jim who taught me the connotative difference between "rabbits" and "rabbit." Big Jim loves "rabbit," and helps us deal with the problem of over-population from time to time. He had tried in the past to raise his own herd, but the barking of three hundred Old English Sheepdogs proved disruptive to bunny amours.

"I'll give him a hand in a minute," I said,

following the scorched smell into the kitchen. "Coffee first."

"He brought you a little gift."

"He shouldn't have done that."

"You got that right," Topaz said.

Just then the kitchen door sprung open and there was a flurry of paws, tail, and teeth hurtling against my right leg.

"Ain't she a beaut?" said Big Jim, beaming. "Champion stock and already house broke. You won't ever find company as good as an Old English Sheepdog. Why she can go right along with you in the car, little as she is now. You won't even know she's there. Minds too. Look at this. 'Here Alice.' "

"Alice!" Topaz and I said together.

"Knows her name, she does."

Bruce came in and contemplated the puppy with disgust. "They're goin' to get along. I can see that," said Big Jim. "They take to each other."

"Jim —"

"Now I know what you're goin' to say," said Big Jim, holding up a concrete block of a hand. "But you got to try her. I just know you're goin' to love her. And she loves you already. Just look there how she's lickin' your foot."

The phone rang. "You wait here for me Jim," I said, running for the bedroom extension. "Right here."

"Your mother cried all night," said my stepfather.

"Let me talk to her," I said.

"That won't be necessary," he said.

"You called me," I said.

"Well, I have a little favor to ask."

"Now? I'm packing."

"Am I right to assume you need money?"

"I'm fine," I said. "Don't worry."

"What're you living on right now? I'm your father, aren't I?"

I let that one pass.

"I care," he said into the void. After his words had reverberated three or four times across greater Los Angeles he recovered his direction. Sometimes letting people hear their own clichés cures them, but not often. And not in this case.

"Anyway . . . here you can help yourself and me at the same time."

"Enlightened self-interest," I said.

"Whatever. Anyway, I got some boxes I need dropped off for a friend in New Orleans. A hundred bucks a box, up front."

"Your father is a generous man," came my mother's voice from a third telephone.

"How big are the boxes?" I said.

"He's been good to you, Arden."

"Where's Big Jim?" I said, striding back into the living room.

"Gone," said Topaz, who was walking backward through the screen door, balancing Kip's chest of drawers between Tom and himself.

"Gone! Gone!"

"Urgent business, he said. The dog's under Jamie's bed." The door banged shut.

"Hi Tom," I said through the screen door. "Oh, and Topaz . . ."

They paused.

"Pack everything in tight. Shelden's bringing over some boxes he wants dropped off in New Orleans."

"He what!"

"Boxes," I said, disappearing into the house. "Four boxes."

In Jamie's room I stretched out on my belly and looked under her bed. Two shining eyes looked back. "Alice?" I said.

The phone rang. I scrambled to my feet, ran into my room, yanked up the princess receiver as if it were the cause of all my woes. "Hello," I growled.

"Arden?"

"Alice?"

"This is Monica," said Monica, politely ignoring my mistake. "How are you?"

"I'm packing," I said inhospitably.

"I know this is a really terrible time to call," she said. "And I want you to know you can say no. I mean I've always felt we could be friends, or that we were friends and that if either of us needed the other to tell the absolute truth then we would. The fact is, I'm leaving town. I've decided to go home until I can sort things out."

I sank onto the bed.

"And I was wondering if I could catch a ride with you and Topaz as far as New Orleans. That is, if there's room."

In the split second before I agreed, I saw a bright blue biplane with sequined tap dancers all struggling to load onto the wings four giant boxes, an Old English Sheepdog, and Malthus' former fiancée.

* * * * *

177

I adjusted my rearview mirror, placing Monica dead center. At the back of the hearse she sat on the floor, propped from behind by Shelden's wall of boxes, on one side by my duffel bag, and the other by a huge box of stuffed animals. She dozed and the dog dozed in her lap. Topaz turned in the passenger seat for a look.

"She acts like somebody recovering from heart surgery," he said, easing back around.

"That's a fair description of her recent life," I said, glancing sidelong out the window at acres and acres of sand. "Do you mind her coming?"

"Well . . . let's just say I was looking forward to not being anybody's mother for a week or two."

"I think she has a mother. In New Orleans."

"She does look just a tad like Shirley Temple, though. Curly Top. This bears watching. Shirley Temple is always on the lookout for a dad who tap dances."

"And a curly dog with a woeful expression, if memory serves."

"Just such a one," said Topaz. "A dog named Alice."

As if in reply, Alice lifted her tiny muzzle and cried. "She must want out," said Monica.

"Why not?" said Topaz. "That's what she wanted in Culver City, that's what she wanted in West Covina, San Berdoo, Pomona, Cucamonga, Palm Springs, Indio . . ."

"I'll take her," I said, slowing down and pulling onto the shoulder.

"I don't mind," Monica said. "I'll take the dog."

It was as if Monica had said, "Sit!" in a kindly but firm tone. We sat. We watched the two orphans trudge out into the sand, their footprints slowly filling in behind them.

I don't really know why I chose the Space Age Motel. Maybe all that sand had left my reasoning capacity impaired. Or maybe Topaz's macabre interest in a grim little mom-and-pop motel on the outskirts of Red Rock made me a trifle uneasy. Unaccountably I found myself saying, "That one. The one with the rocket ship next to the pool."

At any rate, here we were in the Space Age Motel. Topaz was watching a Doris Day movie on TV, Monica was — of course — walking the dog, and I was soaking in the bathtub. After the narrow brush with the Bates Motel, I was not about to risk a shower.

I had delayed contemplating the desert in its metaphoric glory until safely submerged in water. Driving, I had let the whole panorama roll past me like a cheap stage-setting. All that chaparral and those Indian rocks; sun and shadow. All that space and emptiness. I had known, if I had let myself, that I would begin to feel I was staring out the eye-hole of one of Georgia O'Keeffe's cow skulls. There was something dead and artful about the whole thing.

"Topaz," I called. "Are you there?"

"Course I'm here. Where else would I be?"

"I was just thinking."

"Oh, oh. That's bad."

"Do you think Monica's all right out in the desert by herself?"

"Okay, I hear you. But you get out of that tub and keep your eye on Rock Hudson till I get back."

"Thanks," I said, standing, wrapping myself in a space-age towel. I slipped into my pajamas and sat on the foot of the nearest bed. Doris Day and Rock Hudson were arguing in theirs, though theirs lacked the distinctive Star Trek motif ours bore. Doris Day looked like a drag queen.

There was a pounding on the door. I pushed aside the meteorite drapes and looked through the front window. There stood Topaz with a picnic hamper on one arm and Monica on the other.

I opened the door. "I thought you were the police," I said.

"No, but don't dismiss the possibility. We got some pretty funny looks out there."

"Out where?"

"The geriatric set by the pool. Well, think about it. A red-haired woman walks out into the desert at night. She's got this picnic hamper on her arm. She stands there a long time saying every now and then, "That's good Alice." Then a black man comes out. They walk back together . . ."

"It's beautiful out there, Arden," Monica said, letting Alice out of the hamper. "So cool. And the stars . . ."

I shivered.

"Cold?" asked Monica. "Your hair's wet." She touched my head lightly. I grabbed my towel and began a flurry of drying.

"So," said Topaz, "was he unfaithful or not?"

"Who?" Monica and I said in unison.

"Rock Hudson, of course. What he sees in Doris Day I'll never know. Anybody want a beer?"

I took one and Monica went to shower. Topaz stretched out on one of the beds. "Oh Christ. Have you tried the goddamned beds? Let me see this one. No, it's the same. Try this."

I stretched out on the vacant one and promptly rolled straight into the middle. "I can't sleep with Monica on this. We'll be rolling into each other. I'm a married woman."

"Not exactly," said Topaz gently.

"I'll sleep with you," I said.

"I beg your pardon."

"May I? I mean, Tom wouldn't mind, would he?"

"Not in this lifetime." He laughed, pulling me into a sitting position. "But I'm a queen-size kind of a guy and this is a double bed."

"Is that what it is? I didn't think they made them anymore." I looked over at the TV. Rock and Doris were snuggled into a queen-size Posturepedic, their heads resting on pillows as big as concrete sacks. They smirked and turned off the lights.

"Isn't that disgusting," I said. "Heterosexuals are so smug."

"Well," said Topaz, pursing his lips and raising his voice two octaves, "I wouldn't mind if they did it in the privacy of their own homes. But when they begin to invade the living room of the American family with their trash . . ."

"Oh," said Monica, emerging in a cloud of steam, "I thought someone was here."

"More or less," said Topaz. "Done with the shower?"

When he had closed the door behind him, Monica came over and sat next to me on the bed. She was wearing a pink night shirt and smelled of motel soap. "I hope I haven't offended Topaz."

"He likes to growl is all. We'll all feel better after a good night's sleep. Leaving people behind is never easy."

"I *am* tired," she said. "Are we sharing a bed?"

"I'll be with Topaz."

"He's awfully big."

"Oh we've managed before," I lied. "Camping with the kids."

"Well then, I think I'll get comfortable."

"Good luck," I said, just before she tumbled into the middle of her bed.

She lay there for a moment, silent. Then she laughed softly. "Do you know there are actually planets and stars on the ceiling?"

I looked up. There they were, silver foil stars and planets peeling at the edges, scattered on a galaxy of water-stained ceiling tiles.

I slept but ill that night. Topaz tumbled into the bed's pit early on. Expecting the worst, I had taken the precaution of hitching myself to one side of the mattress with my right leg and so had escaped being crushed. I felt like Ahab stuck fast to Moby Dick by stray harpoons.

I looked down at Topaz. The fierceness of my gaze must have penetrated into his unconscious; he decided to sleep on his back. One long arm flung skyward, then dropped directly on my nose.

"Ouch!"

"Arden, Arden," came a soft voice. "Are you all right?"

"Topaz has broken my nose." I slid down off the mattress and headed for the bathroom.

Monica met me with a fistful of Kleenex. "Here, tilt your head back." Then I could hear her rummaging for ice in the cooler. She held an ice-filled towel against the back of my head. We stood silent listening to a toilet flushing somewhere overhead, an engine starting in the parking lot. Finally she said, "Wait here."

She was pulling the mattress onto the floor, working almost soundlessly. Alice whimpered. Topaz moaned once. "Come now. We should have done this hours ago." She held the covers for me. I slipped inside and instantly felt my spine relax. "I'll be right back," she whispered.

I put my hand where I thought she'd be. "Don't go," I said. "It isn't safe. The dog can wait."

She took my hand. "It'll just be a minute. Then she'll settle down."

I listened to the rattle of the chain being released, the inward squeak of door, the solid closing. "I'm afraid,' I said to the sleeping room.

A few minutes later the door opened again, then shut against the desert. Monica got into bed quietly. To the sound of her soft breathing I fell asleep at last.

CHAPTER 22:
Breaking Bread

"Come in under the shadow of this Red Rock," I said, biting into a dusty Egg McNothing.

"Don't get literary," said Topaz, reading the tiny print on his syrup container. "I hate it when you get literary in the morning. And what's potassium sorbate anyway?"

"I think it's used in dry-cleaning fluid," Monica said matter-of-factly.

"You are *both* lots of fun in the morning." Topaz poured the potassium sorbate on his pancakes with the air of someone who no longer cared if he lived or died.

"I had a dream," I said.

"Please don't tell it," Topaz pleaded. "You know I hate to hear other people's dreams."

"This was a voice dream."

"What's a voice dream?" asked Monica.

Topaz groaned.

"In a voice dream you see nothing. Maybe a little cloud or mist, or maybe nothing at all. But there's a large voice. Authoritative, you know. This one said: 'MUCH OF TEXAS IS IRRELEVANT.' "

"Fear of the Permian Basin," Topaz diagnosed. "But you got to get hold of yourself. We got three days' worth of Texas facing us." He sketched the figure 3 into the pool of toxic syrup on his Styrofoam plate. "But we ain't never stopping at no Permian Basin. You got that?"

"We shouldn't be eating here," said Monica. "They use Styrofoam."

"The pancakes were Styrofoam, I can tell you that." Topaz leaned back, held his stomach, and groaned. "I'll never dance again."

There was a puffy family at the table opposite. The boy was trying to keep two straws from falling out of his nostrils. His sister kept jostling his elbow. Mom was building a Styrofoam tower. They must have had two breakfasts apiece, judging by its height. Dad tenderly lifted the greasy column and bore it unsteadily toward McTrash.

Topaz looked up and shuddered. Monica went to walk Alice. I spread out the map to find McTexas.

* * * * *

I sat on the bed in the Muleshoe Motel in Mesquite, Texas, listening to the phone ring at home eight hundred miles away.

At last someone picked it up. "Wicks residence," said the voice. "Ruth Sharp speaking."

I froze, but the operator had the presence of mind to identify herself and me, and to ask if someone there would pay for the call.

There was a long pause during which you could hear cosmic tumbleweeds blowing through space.

At last the resident orphan said, "Yes, of course."

"Ruth," I said, "may I speak to Alice."

"What a shame," said Ruth insincerely, "you just missed her. She and Kip went out not five minutes ago to pick up a pizza. Would you like to leave a message?"

I thought of several. "Just tell her I'm in Texas."

"Texas?"

"Yes, deep in the heart." I hung up.

Topaz dumped our luggage on the bed opposite. "You can't blame Alice just because she happened not to be home when you called."

"I know that," I said.

"Here now." Topaz took Alice's wiggling namesake out of the picnic hamper and put her in my arms.

"It's not the same," I said. "I need Mexican food."

"It'll be Tex-Mex," he warned.

"Whatever."

* * * * *

El Arroyo was dim inside. We followed a young man dressed in white linen through a candle-lit maze of dark, heavy tables and ladder-back leather chairs. The walls were covered with a mural that seemed a replica of the terrain we had passed through that day: salt plains, irrigated desert, mountains. Behind our booth were painted three goats who stared down at our table as if they were trying to read the menus over our shoulders.

"Esperanza will serve you," said the young man. He disappeared into the side of a mountain.

Like all people with allegorical names, Esperanza seemed far from hopeful. I had known in my time an agnostic Faith, a reckless Prudence, and a selfish Charity.

"We're all out of the carne asada," she told Topaz with a dour expression. "I could check but it wouldn't do any good."

"Let's all have a Margarita," I suggested, "while we look at the menu."

"You can't have frozen," said Esperanza with the first hint of a smile. "The blender is broken."

"Just run them under the broiler," said Topaz through clenched teeth.

"The broiler?"

"He's joking," I said. "On the rocks will be fine."

"I feel somebody staring," said Monica, unfolding the thick napkin in her lap.

"I think it's the goats," I said, indicating with my shoulder the portrait behind us.

"Oh my," said Monica. "I hope Alice will be all right."

"Alice?" I said.

"I took her out just before we left," said Topaz.

"But they are staring. People, I mean. They've been staring at us for almost a thousand miles.

"They must be exhausted," I said, picking up my menu.

"Now I know you don't like to hear this, Arden. But we are in the South. South as in Baptist? You know what I'm saying?"

"I know what you're saying, yes. But what's that got to do with how we live our lives? Let them stare. We're going to go about our business until we can't go any further because of armed tanks. Then I get out my flame-thrower and not a minute before."

Esperanza, eavesdropping on my last sentence, set down our drinks carefully and with a new respect. "You folks decided yet?"

"I'll have the cabrito," said Topaz with a snort.

"What's cabrito?" asked Monica.

"Goat," I said.

"Baby goat," corrected Esperanza.

"Give me the same," Monica said, looking steadily at Topaz.

"I'll have the albondigas soup and a chili relleno when you bring the goats," I said, handing Esperanza the three oversized menus.

"I'm gong to call Tom," Topaz said, rising. "I want to tell him what a scintillating time I'm having in beautiful, downtown Mesquite."

I glanced about the room uneasily, feeling the accusing gaze of the goats boring into the back of my neck. Monica was staring at a cow's skull painted on the opposite wall.

Then the melancholic Esperanza slid my soup between my elbows and sighed audibly. "Thanks," I said, staring into my soup.

188

Now this soup spoke to me. Though I had been vaguely troubled at El Arroyo's paucity of Naugahyde, nevertheless the opaque crescents of simmered celery floating docilely near a bed of fresh cilantro suggested authenticity. I intruded my nose into the cloud of steam and inhaled. Then I plunged my big spoon into that healing soup. Cow skulls and other images of death receded from my view as I spooned my way eagerly toward warmth and health. It was *sabrosa*.

But Monica was speaking, had been speaking, was saying now — what was it? — that people, she had read somewhere, who liked to eat, generally enjoyed sex.

My spoon, accidentally striking the bowl like a gong, sounded its alarm as far as the kitchen, from which Esperanza emerged as if summoned, her dark eyebrows raised in questioning.

I went to a psychic once who was famous for discovering truth by rocking vigorously in a squeaking rocking chair. In my case she finally ceased her exertions and asked in desperation, "Do you read a lot?" I think she was picking up interference from the customary uproar going on deep inside my head where all the people I have ever read or read about live, talk, and laugh with one another during all my waking moments and sometimes my sleeping ones too.

Competing with this racket that fiction tends to generate is the noise my mind makes when it is sorting uneasily or joyfully through my past. Alice used to call this part of my mind The Rag And Bone Shop.

Lying sleepless that night in the Muleshoe Motel in Mesquite, Texas, I tried to turn down the volume in my mind so that Monica, lying next to me, would nod off to sleep in the middle of the *Maltese Falcon* as Topaz had done earlier in the middle of *To Catch a Thief.*

Monica's freshly shampooed strawberry locks were so near my face I could feel the dampness. I was trying to remember where in medieval literature I had read about two people sleeping in the same bed with a sword between them. A naked sword, actually. Somehow a naked sword sounded a whole lot more erotic than the other kind. I tried not to dwell on the nakedness but just on the safe feeling this sword presumably gave everybody concerned. I lay very still to convince Monica I was asleep and to convince myself I was not the passionate creature my eating style suggested I was.

Quietly I searched among the several thousand characters who had taken up housekeeping in my mind. Certainly sleep was out of the question until I matched up the sword image with the people in bed with it. At the same time I tried counting backwards, mimicking the voice from a relaxaation tape I used to have. But the numbers turned into sheep and then into sheepdogs and eventually into goats. Tender ones. I was stuck midway between alarm and sleep when Monica finally spoke.

"Arden," she whispered into my right ear. There was no choice but to breathe in her Ultress and be damned.

Suddenly a glowing sword appeared between us. Very sharp. "Don't cut yourself," I said.

"Are you awake?"

"Not yet," I said, floating toward a waterfall of discovery or sleep.

"I was wondering how people can tell when they're in love with somebody."

"Tristan," I said into her curls. "It was Tristan and Isolde in a motel bed. In Texas, I think. Must have been."

Topaz sat up in bed. "I can't sleep when you do that Arden. You're asleep and you know it."

I rolled over very carefully and turned out my lights.

CHAPTER 23:
Pressed Flowers

"Well ma'am," said Topaz to the mistress of Kabin Kuntry in Mountain Home, Texas, "I guess our money spends as good as anybody else's."

She and her apricot poodle were eyeing us suspiciously through the drive-up window. The artificial light behind them lit up their faces strangely, as if they were about to sing an aria. They both had dark circles under their eyes and wore magenta nail polish. "You'll need to pay in advance," she said, "naturally."

"Naturally," I said, placing my Visa card into her slide-out drawer. She and her partner disappeared from the window. "Do you think she's gone to call the Vice Squad?"

"They certainly are friendly folk in Mountain Home," said Topaz.

"Maybe they have to be careful," said Monica.

"If we all had orange hair they wouldn't have to be careful, you can bet your sweet ass."

"Topaz," I said.

"Oh, don't pay me no never mind, honey. I was just wishing to Miss Monica here I was born an apricot poodle."

"You've got no right," said Monica in an even tone, "to talk to me like that."

Alice growled from inside her hamper.

"She's going to bark," I said, "and so am I."

"Welcome to Kabin Kuntry," said its proprietress grimly. The little drawer slid out abruptly into the rearview mirror. "Sign by the X and be sure to write down your phone number and address, if you got any. You're in number seven."

"No thumb print?" mumbled Topaz.

"What was that, young man?"

"He said, 'Kabin Kuntry,' ma'am. He loves the rustic life."

"I was born in a kabin," said Topaz.

I waved, shifted into first gear, and headed out into the piney darkness. We bumped along a rutted dirt road, the trailer yanking from time to time against its hitch. Eventually we spotted a light fixed to a telephone pole, and behind that a log cabin with a front porch. Mounted on the front door was a pink and blue plaque saying, Heidi #1.

"Oh Christ," said Topaz, "I forgot my lederhosen."

About half a mile further on we came to Hans #3. Then Fritz #5.

"What happened to Gretel #1 and Frankenstein #4?"

"They're all irrational numbers," Monica observed. Topaz groaned and Alice growled.

"Here we are," I said, pulling up in front of Gretchen #7.

Monica opened the hamper lid and the car door. Soon Alice was scampering in circles and barking for joy. Inside we found a kitchenette and four bunk beds. There was a broken-down couch and a daddy chair in matching motel plaid. Tiny reading lamps were clamped onto the upper bunks.

I threw my bag onto one. "May I?" I asked.

"Yes you may. But Gretchen seems to be missing one small amenity," Topaz said, throwing his duffel bag onto a lower bunk.

"No TV," said Monica, who obviously had grown up in Mr. Rogers' neighborhood.

"You tell her," gasped Topaz.

"Tell me what?"

"There's no bathroom," I said.

"Of course there's a bathroom." She yanked open the closet door.

"I think I'll go call Tom," Topaz said. Monica's eyes hastily swept the room for the telephone. "And

I'll pick up a pizza or something. Greasy fried chicken would be nice."

"I'll cook," I said. "Get some fish."

"I don't think they have fish in Texas."

"And toilet paper."

Topaz left the room chanting "Fish and toilet paper, fish and toilet paper . . ."

The door to the outhouse bore a little blue plaque that said BUCKS AND DOES. Monica called from inside that everything was actually very clean and as long as she breathed through her mouth she was fine. I scuffed around in the pine needles for a while, enjoying the way the last light in summer always makes things stand out in distinct but soft outline. It almost seemed that through the opening in the pine forest we should be able to see the ocean.

"Which ocean?" asked Monica, zipping up her pants, the door banging behind her.

"You caught me thinking there's only one," I laughed. "For me it's the Pacific. You're a Gulf person, I guess."

She fell into step behind me. "I like these long days. It feels lazy here. I wish . . ."

"Wish what?"

"That this was our home and we'd live here always."

"Well, I believe we will. I think sometimes — when the light is just right — a moment becomes so drenched with essence that clocks stop, shaping a lovely place in time that afterwards we can visit, as if the place becomes actual and permanent, like a wildflower pressed in a book."

"You really are a poet — aren't you? — an artist."

We climbed the three steps up the porch and sat down in the swing, as if by agreement.

"Yes, but I might not mean it the way you do. To me everybody's an artist."

She turned and looked at me, then away into the woods.

"What is your art?" I asked her, trying to make the question sound lighter than it was.

"I've been thinking about that," she said. "On this trip. Wondering what it is I'll do when I get home. You're lucky to know."

"That's one value the Gridleys of the world have."

"No, I mean your poetry. Writing is what you do, like breathing. I want to do something that's no different than breathing." She held out her hands, and made a kind of sliding motion with her left, as if these were not hands at all but dancers. "I want to make pots, mugs, plates, vases. Things that people will hold, eat from, drink from, break and mend. I'm going to do that."

I gave a little shiver.

"This trip has helped, but I've really known since I was eight. It was my Aunt Julia's doing. She took me to Newcomb College on the bus, one of our many field trips together." Monica closed her eyes for help. "I remember the buildings, tall and white and cool inside. For a while the women had actually lived here. Inside were blue and green pottery-filled shelves,

196

book cases, table tops. It was everywhere and all of it different but somehow the same. Beautiful flowing shapes painted with flowers, turtles, houses, fish, foxes in clothes. Thick glazes. Everywhere we could feel the presence of these women, these artists, and the energy they left behind in the chairs they sat in, the lamps they lit, even in the walls. Their pottery was more alive than most living people. How could I have forgotten all those years? What was I doing marrying Malthus!"

"My sweet friend," I said, taking her potter's hands into my own, "you are talking about art but you are also talking about the power in a community of women."

Just then we saw Topaz's blue fender coming into view. He was back from his phone call and his shopping. There was something about the way he set the hand brake, though, the careful way he shut the car door, not looking at us. And when he came up the stairs, he carried nothing.

"Arden," he said, bending over me and running his hands down my shoulders and arms, "you need to call Alice. There's trouble. Ruby had a stroke. She died last night."

"My Ruby?" I asked, looking up into his face.

I set out running for the motel office. "I told her you were coming," Topaz called after me. His voice sounded far away, like a voice from a dead star. Several minutes passed before I realized Topaz meant the hotel clerk, and not Ruby. I heard a gasping sound come from my chest and then only the sound of my own feet beating on the dirt road like a terrified heart. Light from the nearly full moon lit up the trunks of the pines. Somehow I missed the main road, had to circle back, finally saw neon winking KOZY KABIN, the flashing arrow pointing my way to the office door.

"My friend," I panted to the back-lit form framed in the screen door, "she died."

"I'm Mrs. Rhodes," she said, opening the screen door with one hand and gesturing me in with the hand holding the apricot poodle. Then she led me down a narrow hall and into her living quarters. A swamp cooler blew moist air. She motioned me into a deep chair and slid up close a tiny table that held a telephone. Suddenly I was alone with the phone. I took a deep breath and dialed.

"Alice?"

"Yes, dear. I'm so sorry. Topaz told you?"

"I can't believe it. Should I —"

"No dear. She didn't want a service. Honey will scatter her ashes from an airplane. Over the bay, I think she said. We didn't know how to call you."

"Is Honey all right?"

"I think so. They have friends there."

I slapped my pockets for a Kleenex. Mrs. Rhodes emerged from the hall and placed a box on my knees and then disappeared again.

"She was only seventy-four, for Christ's sake," I said into the Kleenex.

"What, dear?" said Alice.

"I said that seventy-four years is not long enough. In Ruby's case."

"Yes, love."

"She was in perfect health."

"Not quite," said Alice gently.

I tried to feel the rhythm of Alice's breathing over the phone lines, to tune my lungs and heart to hers.

"You are very sane," I told Alice.

"And you have a great heart."

"It feels right now exactly like that ashtray I made in first grade."

"The one we keep tiny, gold safety pins in?"

"Yes," I said, "the one with the crazed lines running all over it from being fired imperfectly. That's how my heart looks."

"And yet," said my Alice, "it's perfectly serviceable."

"You don't think it's been weakened along the crack lines?"

"Strengthened."

"Did you tell the kids?"

"They're all right. They miss you though. Want to talk to anybody?"

"Tomorrow night. I'll call."

"Good," she said, "that'll be good." Then there was a fifteen-hundred-mile silence. "I don't want to tell you good night. I want very much to hold you. Because I love you and because there's going to be a bit more cracking tonight just before you fall asleep."

"I'll be all right," I said.

"Yes," she said. "And you'll call tomorrow."

After we said good night, I sat in Mrs. Rhodes' chair, staring into her empty fireplace and letting the hum of the swamp cooler enter my soul.

I was startled by a voice at my left elbow. It belonged to a teen-age girl about Jamie's age. She slid a glass of milk and a plate bearing two cookies onto the tiny table. "Granny's idea," she said, flinging herself into the La-Z-Boy opposite and flipping her legs into the air, then freezing them with the lever. "She always thinks people want to eat when folks

199

die. When my mother died I never ate a thing for two weeks. Like to drove Granny wild." She snorted at the thought.

"Courtney," said Mrs. Rhodes, coming into the room in a pale pink chenille robe and her hair in pink rollers. "Mind your manners. This lady's suffered a loss." Then, like trained acrobats, Courtney's legs fell earthward and she rose out of the La-Z-Boy, moving to a side chair the twin of the one I sat in, while Mrs. Rhodes glided into the La-Z-Boy and installed herself in it. The apricot poodle then leapt into her lap, twirled twice, and plunged into sleep.

"I'm an orphan," said Courtney.

"Be careful what you say," said Mrs. Rhodes. "Besides you can't be an orphan when you got me caring for you day and night." Her sun-freckled hand rested lightly on the rising and falling back of the sleeping dog.

"I'm an orphan," said Courtney, "if my mama's dead and my daddy's run off with some honky-tonk woman."

"You ain't," said Mrs. Rhodes, "and that's that. Let the dead rest in peace."

"My mama died under mysterious circumstances," continued Courtney, "in New Orleans."

"Your mama had been a world better off if she'd learned how to be happy in Mountain Home like I always been," said Mrs. Rhodes. "Ain't nothing missing from Mountain Home that folks truly need."

"There's not one movie house in Mountain Home," said Courtney. "Now can you believe that? This place is not what you could call civilized. My mama wanted to be a star in the pictures, and could of been too, if it hadn't of been for mysterious circumstances. You know what they were?" Courtney leaned close, her eyebrows raised.

"You don't know, missy, and never will either. This lady's got trouble of her own. You got to learn to think about others and keep your family trouble to yourself. Let sleeping dogs lie," she said, glancing down at the poodle in her lap. "Anyway, that's my advice."

"You going to New Orleans?" asked Courtney.

"Yes," I said. "We'll pass through. One of my friends will stay on there. She grew up in New Orleans."

Courtney's eyes widened. "Grew up there!"

"She wants to learn pottery-making."

"My mama went there to learn movies. And she did, too. She was in plenty of movies. Not exactly like Hollywood movies, but movies anyway. And she was an artists' model too. I'm going there one day, you can bet."

"You're just fine where you're at, Courtney Luanne. People who stay in Mountain Home and mind their own bidness don't get in the kind of trouble your mama did. Big cities mean big trouble. Simple as that."

"When are you going there? Tomorrow?" Courtney looked like she might want to add herself to our list of orphans.

"Day after," I said. "Tomorrow we spend in Texas, then New Orleans."

Courtney glanced at her grandmother, then down at her battered Reeboks. "I'm still in school. I'm sorry your friend died. Death is a real bummer." She rose, and disappeared down the dark hall.

I got up and thanked my hostess. She rose, adroitly scooping the poodle onto her shoulder. "I'm sorry about your friend, too. Have a safe journey." She walked me to the office door. "And watch out for snakes." She pressed a flashlight into my hand. "They're out and about now. It's their time."

CHAPTER 24:
Mud

"Rest the *cabeza* on this," said Luna Morales, slipping a folded towel under my head, just as I slid into the mud-filled bathtub in cubicle five of the Sulphur Springs Health Spa. "Ten minutes in here, then you shower off and meet your friends in the mineral pool, then into the cold dip. You're going to feel like a million-dollar bill. You need anything?"

I shook my head.

"It's going to feel longer, but Luna don't forget you." She pulled the door closed and was gone.

I lifted my foot experimentally. There was a sucking sound. My foot was coated in gray. I returned it to the muck. Obviously a death symbol. Or was it a life symbol?

Pots were made from clay like this. Newcomb pottery. I wanted to be thrown on a wheel by the goddess, reshaped, and painted in earth tones.

But first I wanted to shut my mind down for the ten minutes Luna was giving me, to drift undirected, unanalytical, without metaphor. I wanted to visit the dead and kiss their feet, to offer them something not available in death, something simple, a piece of fruit, a song.

Oh Ruby! Here I am, mired in mud, remembering you and Aunt Vi in Mexico, how you stood watching the vermilion sunsets, how you walked the long beach, leaning toward each other in your rambling talks, simple women loving each other simply.

"Alice," I said out loud, "don't leave me!"

The words hung in the air like subtitles to a foreign movie. I looked about me with absolute determination, trying to grasp the solidity of the room — the shape of its whitewashed adobe bricks, the layers of dust defining each brick, showing it distinct from all others, the slatted wooden bench with my jeans and shirt and underwear laid across, my sandals underneath, darkened inside with the pattern of my daily feet, the concrete floor, its rosy patina, its fretwork of cracks, the smell of mud and whiffs of sulphur. Had I said those words, those hanging suspended?

"Ah," I said to Death, "*thou* shalt die."

CHAPTER 25:
Second Lining

I let my head loll back against the pillow we kept atop one of Shelden's boxes and stretched my legs forward until they touched Hillary's box of stuffed animals. It felt wonderfully cozy in the back of the hearse, with summer rain pelting us slantwise, turning our world silver. There was something exhilarating about not being in Texas anymore but instead heading along the Pontchartrain Expressway toward New Orleans and the Marie Laveau Guest House.

Monica was driving because this was home to her, and Topaz slouched against the passenger window, dozing. In the rearview mirror I could see the soft curve of Monica's chin, framed by a deep green Mercedes. In my mind I took a farewell snapshot for safekeeping. The way to love Monica was at a distance. It was time to sleep alone and call my children home.

"Do you see it too?" asked Monica, catching my eye in the rearview mirror.

"See what?" The rain was letting up, but there was still a cloud of moisture hovering.

"What?" said Topaz, jerking himself erect.

"That car, the green Mercedes," Monica said. "Don't turn around. I think it's following us."

We rode for some time, our heads facing forward like crash dummies. Then Topaz turned half around, as if to speak casually to me, his arm resting on the back of the seat.

"If this were my little theory you'd have said I was being paranoid again," he remarked out of the corner of his mouth. "Lucky Monica here has red hair and is straight. We can rely on her as a reality check."

"I'm not straight," said Monica, changing lanes.

Topaz shook his head. "You white folks got the strangest sense of timing. No wonder you can't dance."

"What are we going to do?" I asked.

"You mean about Monica?"

"I mean about this green car. A plan, we need a plan."

"Let's flush them into the open," Monica said, suddenly crossing two lanes in time to catch an off-ramp.

"Is this wise?" said Topaz, scrunching down into his seat.

"They're following," said Monica.

She began weaving her way into the French Quarter, but apparently following a pattern of some kind, as if she were searching for a drowned person at the bottom of a dark lake. Expertly she wheeled us left, then right, right, then left. I looked into street-corner faces, with their deep curious eyes trying to see through the windows' tint at the corpse that might be concealed inside the strange visiting hearse. At last we stopped in a narrow side street, where Monica pulled car and trailer up to the curb. The green Mercedes slowly passed, carrying two balding heads off down the street and out of sight.

"Café du Monde," said Monica. We sprung open three doors, and walked to the end of the street where we found both the Mississippi and a large open air cafe canopied in striped, flapping canvas. We settled ourselves in dampish campaign chairs and picked up sticky menus behind which we could keep watch for balding heads.

The first one we spied belonged to a small, energetic waiter wearing a large white apron. Monica ordered café au lait all around and a plate of beignets.

"I hate milk in my coffee," said Topaz.

"You'll like this," Monica said in a tone between prediction and warning. "It's got chicory."

"I hate chicory even more than milk."

The waiter returned and slipped paper placemats

in front of us. They were decorated with a map of the quarter and a gigantic Café du Monde planted between Jackson Square and the Riverwalk.

"Here they come," said Monica. "Don't look."

Instead we looked at Monica. She opened her blue eyes very wide, then made them tremble and quiver as if they were going to leap out of their sockets.

We both laughed, snorted, grabbed for water glasses. "How do you do that?" gasped Topaz.

"It's like wiggling your ears," she said.

"Go ahead, wiggle them," challenged Topaz. Whereupon Monica obliged, and the waiter had to risk life and limb setting down three cups of café au lait and a white mountain of beignets before us. Topaz took a sip of coffee and smiled approval.

"They're sitting at a table behind Topaz's head," Monica said.

"Who?" we both asked.

"The bald men," she answered, sending a puff of confectioners sugar into the air.

"That's all very hard to believe," I said, smacking my lips and enjoying the sudden appearance of the sun. "Personally I have an enormous sense of well-being."

"And that mood," said Topaz to Monica, "usually is a prelude to disaster. What're they doing now?"

"One of them is ordering. The other got up a moment ago and disappeared."

"Maybe he went to the can," Topaz said, carefully selecting another beignet.

"Maybe he's making a phone call to Mr. Big," I said.

"Maybe they're putting a contract out on us,"

said Monica. "Oh, here he comes. Now he's sitting down, leaning forward to say something. No. The waiter just came back. He's putting down cups of coffee. They're sitting there as if they'd never laid eyes on each other in their lives."

I watched a paddle wheel steamer move across the horizon. "Still," I said, "it's a lovely day. And Monica's going to see her mother and her aunt. And Topaz, you and I get to spend the night at Marie Laveau's Guest House."

"Voodoo," said Monica. "They say she was a voodoo princess."

Topaz began humming "You Do Something to Me" and tapping out a time-step under the table. A seagull landed by my foot and speared an abandoned beignet.

Then Monica suddenly looked at Topaz, or past him. "Don't turn around," she said without moving her lips. "They're paying their check."

I picked up our own greasy, powdery check, then laid a ten-dollar bill on it.

"You can look now, slowly." The two men had moved onto the sidewalk, walking close to the buildings. Then they turned down the street where we had parked the rig.

When we got to the corner, one bald man was trying to jimmy the lock on the driver's side of the hearse while the other sat at the wheel of the green car with the passenger door open and the engine running, small clouds of diesel exhaust chuffing out the tailpipe.

Topaz took off running, whisper silent, toward them, with Monica and me close behind. The one working on the hearse looked up, gave a yelp, and jumped into the Mercedes. Topaz was there by the time his door slammed. But the window was open. Topaz reached through and pulled the man hard and sudden against the door as if he meant to pull him right through. But the car had begun moving, Topaz running sideways now, still yanking on the man, until he could no longer keep up.

Inside the hearse, Alice was barking. Monica tried the driver's door and it swung open. Alice jumped into her arms. Topaz still stood in the middle of the street, hands on his hips. Slowly he walked back toward us. Then he stopped and yelled, "Fuck, fuck, fuck!"

An old black woman came out on the balcony above, leaned on the wrought iron railing and said, "You should be shamed a yourself."

"Oh I am," said Topaz, looking up. "I truly am." He smiled, she gave a quick nod and went back inside. "Did you check the trailer lock?" he asked me.

"It's okay but the lock on the driver's door is gone."

"Shit," said Topaz under his breath, and climbed into the back of the car.

Monica had gone to walk Alice. I slipped into the driver's seat and pulled the door closed. It wouldn't stay shut. "Shit," I said.

"Exactly," said Topaz, leaning his head back against the boxes and examining his hands. "Son of a bitch scratched me. Like a fucking cat."

Monica got in the passenger seat with Alice. "I don't understand this. What could they possibly want? Arden's furniture? The children's clothes?"

"Maybe Alice is a very valuable dog," I said,

rummaging around in the glove compartment for something to tie the door closed.

Topaz shifted around uncomfortably, then slid one of the boxes over to prop his arm on, then said, "Arden, what the hell's in these boxes Shelden paid us to deliver?"

"I don't know," I said, meeting his eyes. Then I threw a leg over the front seat and rolled down onto the box of stuffed animals.

"Knife," he said, slapping his pockets. Then we began ripping through with our bare hands.

"Sweet Jesus!" Topaz said, sitting back on his heels.

"What is it! Tell me!" said Monica. "It's drugs, isn't it?"

"Actually," I said, "it's bears. Gray teddy bears wearing bow ties." I handed her one.

Topaz took out it's twin. "Bears. Why would anybody pay four hundred dollars to ship four boxes of bears to New Orleans from Southern California?"

"They wouldn't," I said, grabbing another bear. "Nobody would. So they're not really bears."

"Look again," said Topaz wearily. "I guess I know a bear when I see one."

"Find the knife," I said, "seriously."

"Don't be so rash," said Topaz, feeling under the front seat. "Things usually work out. Now where's your optimism?"

I took the knife and slashed my bear across the head. Tiny beads of Styrofoam flew into the air. "These bears are metaphors," I said. "They carry something inside them." I felt the bear's feet. More tiny beads.

Monica squeezed her bear's head. Topaz took the

knife and slashed his bear horizontally. We dispatched three more bears, then Monica looked up. "That car's driven past us three times."

"The green one?" Topaz asked, gathering himself for violent retaliation.

"No, this one's a gray sedan. Maybe the competition. Keep watching. It'll come by again."

It did. Two people, four doors. We couldn't tell much with the burnt-orange sun reflecting off their windows.

"Time to ask Mother," said Monica, sliding into the driver's seat.

"Mother?" we chorused.

We were moving through heavy traffic now, and foot traffic too, while the streets got narrower and narrower. "That's Jackson Square over there," said Monica, gesturing with her chin. "See the artists sketching?"

"Never mind the points of interest," Topaz said. "That gray car's still following us."

"Yes, I know. But I can lose them here in the Quarter. I don't want anybody to follow us to Mother's house."

"Where's Mother's house?"

"The Garden District," she said, stopping for a red light.

Topaz craned his head out the window. "I got news. The green car's coming out of that side street."

"This must be the chase scene," I groaned.

"Only this one's in slow-mo," said Topaz. "I could get off on a nice fast chase scene, where we plowed

212

into fruit carts and between men carrying plate glass and over people climbing out of manholes. But this? We could travel faster on foot."

"Watch for Preservation Hall on your left," Monica advised.

"Step on it, Monica," Topaz growled.

"You're not a very patient person," said Monica, inching forward.

"I'm having a bad day," said Topaz.

"Really, I don't understand this myself," said Monica. "Traffic's not usually this slow around here, even at rush hour. Maybe there's been an accident."

"Plan B," said Topaz, "we got to move on to Plan B. This one's dead in the water. Monica, I'm starting to think you do not have an executive mind."

"No, Topaz, I do not. Nor do I control the wind and the tides. I'm a simple person trying to help my friends out of their trouble."

We moved forward again, slowly and in silence. "We appreciate it," I said in a voice not quite my own. "You're doing the best you can."

"Ah, that's what it is," said Monica. "Up ahead. It's a funeral. A black jazz funeral. See, the cars have totally stopped now. You can just see the hearse crossing in front of us. People are starting the second lining."

"What's the second lining?" I asked, rolling down my window to hear the band.

"People come out of their houses all along the funeral route and join the procession. See, people are starting now. They're coming out of those apartment buildings. And they're getting out of their cars."

"Leaving them here? In the street?" Topaz asked.

"Everybody does. Nobody minds. See, there are police all around."

"I want to go," I said.

"What about everybody who's following us? We got an obligation to these people, you know."

"I'm second lining," I said. "You coming Monica?"

Monica scooped up Alice. Topaz tied the door shut, muttering under his breath. Monica asked a policeman on a horse if he would keep an eye on the rig for us. He tipped his hat.

We moved forward with the surge of people, falling in place behind the black hearse and the band, which was playing a slow cadenced, mournful song. For a moment I felt irreverent, marching in the funeral cortege of a stranger. Then the drumbeats entered me, like Death himself. And it was Ruby we mourned and all our dead. Slowly we moved, as if in shackles, marching to the dark cadence, to all loss — remote or near. The woman next to me passed a pint bottle wrapped in a crumpled brown bag and gestured to me to drink. Bourbon seared my throat. At her urging I passed it on to Topaz, and he on to Monica, and on. "Now," she said, grabbing my elbow.

The music stopped and the river of people with it. We stood in silence for a moment. Then she handed me a heavy walking stick tied with a wide black streamer. "Shake your stick!" she said. All around me people lifted umbrellas, canes, sticks, lifted them high and shook them defiantly at Death. "Die yourself," we told him.

Then the music jumped alive and people began to hug each other and strut and dance, and joy ran through me like shared bourbon. The woman, taking back her stick, held me close and said into my ear,

"This be the cutting loose time." Then she danced on to Topaz, and then Monica, hugging them, kissing them, then dancing on and on through the celebrating world.

CHAPTER 26:
Bear Facts

"Y'all must be half starved," said Monica's mother, setting on the long mahogany table a bowl of rice and a platter of cajun fried chicken, next to the green salad and corn bread. "Funerals always make me hungry and so does travel." She sat down at the head of the table and lifted a hospitable fork, whereupon we fell on the food like wolves.

"I hope y'all know how grateful I am for all you've done for Monica, not the least of which was busting up her impending marriage."

"Mrs. James," I said, "I hope you don't think —"

"He was an egotistical fool, if you want my opinion. I can't think why Monica ever believed she wanted to marry him. Or any man, for that matter. Julia and I always hoped for better things for Monica."

I looked at Aunt Julia. Topaz looked at Aunt Julia, and then at me. Aunt Julia, a robust woman in her early fifties, smiled.

"You mean —" I stammered.

"I'm the other mother," said Aunt Julia, "yes." She took Monica's hand and patted it.

"I know," said Monica, "that you've both tried to raise me right and you haven't always been pleased with my choices. Or maybe I stopped making choices in an effort to please the world. Anyway, I want you both to know about my happiness. I've decided to be a lesbian potter. I've resolved to go to Newcomb College, Aunt Julia, this spring."

Both women half rose, their faces beaming.

"And this wouldn't be true," she continued, gesturing her mothers back into their chairs, "without Arden. And Topaz. And they're in trouble."

"In trouble!" exclaimed Aunt Julia.

"How can we help?" asked Monica's mother.

"It's a very, very long story," said Topaz, spreading homemade jam onto his fifth piece of corn bread.

"I'll get coffee," said Aunt Julia.

"And I'll bring the pecan pie," said Monica's mother, "and then you can tell us the whole story, start to finish."

When they had disappeared into the kitchen, Topaz turned to me and said, "Now you don't tell it. We'll be here another week, that way. You tell it Monica, briefly and without embellishment. We need to settle this thing and be on the road."

The three of us cleared the table, and when we were all comfortable with our coffee and pie, Monica told the story of our travels with a brevity that took my breath away. Gone were all setting, circumstance, metaphor, and innuendo. What remained were the while bleached bones of the tale. Nevertheless, at the end of it, Monica's mother rose and said she knew exactly the right person to help us, and went off to make some calls.

Aunt Julia led us into a snug living room filled with velvet-covered chairs and small cherry tables. On one wall was a fireplace and on another French doors gave onto a little walled courtyard with a small fountain at the center. Monica and I went into the garden, leaving Topaz behind, deep in conversation with Aunt Julia.

It was humid, but the fountain kept the air moving. Ferns sprouted out of every nook and cranny, moss edged the brick walks, and small trees fluttered their lacy leaves in the light breeze.

"Beautiful," I said, settling into a wrought iron chair.

"You're beautiful," said Monica, taking the chair next to mine.

"Monica," I said, taking her hand in mine, then nestling it with my other, "my heart is old and cracked a thousand ways, and not quite mine to give. Yours is new and unblemished. Match it with a sister heart. I think mine wants some time and solitude."

"Does that mean you don't love me?"

"It means I love you very much. Now let's go in. To say more would just confuse things. Besides, you know I'm a woman of few words."

She laughed her soft laugh. We rose, and I followed her in.

"I believe, dears," Mrs. James said, "your trials are almost over. My friend should be here in half an hour." She sat down next to Aunt Julia and they smiled at each other.

"Good," I said, my mind moving on to the next remaining hurdle. "But I don't know what to do about my mother. Presumably she loves Shelden," I said, "though I've never understood why. Maybe I'll call Alice and ask her what she thinks."

"And tell her you're alive," added Topaz. "She might be wondering."

"You can use the phone in our bedroom," said Aunt Julia.

They had a high, antique mahogany bed with little steps leading up to it. I took the phone off the night stand and sat down on the floor with it. If Ruth answered I would hang up.

"Hello," said my love.

"Alice," I said, "Oh Alice."

"Dear, where are you? Are you all right?"

I filled her in, following as best I could Monica's

example of economy. "Now," I concluded, "I don't know how to break this to my mother. Somehow I don't think a singing telegram would serve."

"Shelden disappeared three days ago. Your mother's called several times."

"Is she —"

"Hysterical? Of course. I told her to come over here and we'd all do our best to take care of her. She'll be here tonight. My guess is Shelden felt the hot breath of justice on his neck and beat it. Anyway, don't feel obliged to save him, or your mother. Just feel obliged to find us a decent house when you get to Florida. One with eight bathrooms."

"Us?" I said.

"I'm on the point of concluding I can't live without you. Things are very bleak when you drop off my horizon. But let me look into the job possibilities and see."

I was holding my breath, when Topaz exploded into the room. "Arden, come look out this window. It's the gray sedan. And you are not going to believe —"

"Topaz," I said, "Alice and I —"

He was gone. "Alice," I said, "my greedy self screams for you. My greedy, impatient self. My best self declares its love and waits."

There was a deep silence over the phoneways and muffled bangs and squeals from Monica's living room. "I'll call you tomorrow from Midway, when we can talk. I love you."

"And I, you," said my Alice.

* * * * *

In the living room stood a tall, slim woman whose hair looked like a piece of topiary; it rose in the shape of a triangle. "Now I know this is not Teddie LaRue," she said, smiling.

"Stash!" I said, embracing her. "Have you met all these people?"

"Well, I just met Topaz and Monica, but I've known Helen and Julia for ages. And I've been following your hearse all morning.

"The bears," I remembered out loud.

"The thugs," said Topaz.

"I had them picked up on suspicion of grand theft auto, the suspects, that is. They'll be out of our way for two or three hours. Plenty of time. We'll get the bears in and see what we can find."

Soon we were all sitting on the living room rug squeezing teddy bear parts. It wasn't until the fourth box that Monica's hands found a lumpy head. Stash opened the cranial cavity carefully and shook out a dozen diamonds the size of marbles. All the bears in the bottom half of the box had these lumps in their heads, but Stash wanted the bears left intact and even returned the diamonds into the first bear's head and sutured it closed.

After we'd finished, we climbed into the velvet chairs while Monica made tea. Topaz cleared his throat, something he often does when he is going to make an inappropriate request. "How much of this little caper can we innocent citizens hear about? I mean, we've got an investment of time and stark fear, and I for one —"

"Wait for me," called Monica from the kitchen. In a moment she appeared with a tray and set down proper china cups on the little mahogany tables, passed around lemons, cream and sugar, linen napkins, then sat down next to Stash.

"What I can tell you," Stash said through sips of tea, "is that you got involved, courtesy of Arden's stepfather, in an elaborate network of drug traffic, payment, and money laundering. There's never been any question of your complicity. But I would like to ask one favor."

Monica poured a little more hot tea into Stash's cup and smiled. She seemed ready to promise her anything.

"I'd like to put the boxes back into your car and have you park it somewhere fairly conspicuous. Where are you staying?"

"They're staying here," said Monica's mother.

"We really couldn't," I said. "We're leaving so early —"

"And it would be better from my point of view," continued Stash, "if they were in the Quarter. The Feds can take over from here, watch the car, and get the suspects with the goods on them. All you would have to do is stay in your room, out of their way."

"Easily done," I said, rising with my cup in my hand. "This day has been three weeks long." I made for the kitchen, with Monica right behind.

"Couldn't we have dinner? Or breakfast?" she said.

I set the cup down and took hers out of her hand and placed it beside mine. "Dear," I said, "this won't get any easier, and it might even get worse." I put my arms around her and held her close. "Let me leave you here with your family." Then I kissed her with all the tenderness and exhaustion that was in me.

CHAPTER 27:
Dead Reckoning

Two hours later I was floating in the oversized, footed bathtub belonging to room three-fourteen of the Marie Laveau Guest House. A big pink bar of soap reclined in a wire soap holder suspended from the shoulder of the tub. The heat and steam had made me deliciously muzzy, and I half-believed I had traveled all this way from Los Angeles to New Orleans in a bathtub.

Through the door I could hear Topaz talking long

distance to Tom. It was a low, sweet hum as of bees to flowers. And I began remembering my way backward through the jazz funeral, and the beignets, and the mud bath, through Mountain Home and Courtney, whose mother had vanished somehow in this very city, and Ruby, gone too but somehow still here — "Here," I said out loud, smacking my chest through the water. And then there were tears sliding down my face and dropping into the bath and I closed my eyes.

Later we called room service and ate red snapper sitting on the beds watching *Casablanca*.

"I don't even care," said Topaz, laying down his fork and knife across his empty plate, "that this coffee I am about to drink costs three dollars and seventy-five cents. Everything is worth it."

"How's Tom?" I asked.

"You caught me, didn't you? Optimism. A dead giveaway." He fell back on the bed, laughing. Then he sat up. "Let's have some champagne sent up. Let's celebrate."

By the time the dishes were cleared and the champagne poured, Bogie had watched Ingrid's plane disappear into the gray and white uncertain future. Next came *Seven Brides for Seven Brothers*. Topaz fell asleep during the choreographed house-raising, and I must have dozed off soon after. Inside my head, inside what was not exactly a dream, I heard a sound, a kind of deep boomeranging sound like a communication through vibration, a cosmic mousetrap set off in the night.

I went to the French doors and stepped quietly out onto the tiny balcony. Below in the dim street I could see that the front door of the hearse was open and men were walking away in twos, like partners in a curious square dance. They all got into two cars; you could see them under the dome lights. Then the lights went off; a man from the first car got out and walked over to the hearse, softly closed the door against its broken latch, and walked back. Then two engines started, four headlights cut the damp air, and slowly the cortege moved down the street and out of sight like a stain disappearing.

I breathed deep, listening intently for sounds of the ordinary, calling them up from the restaurant down the street, the rattle of silverware, the clink of glasses set into the dishwasher, the drift of jukebox tunes from the corner bar, a heavy car passing below, its tires sucking softly on asphalt. Leaning back, I looked skyward, scanning the darkness for polestar, North Star, constellations to steer by, galaxies blown into orbit by the divine imagination. My hands gripped the iron railing and I leaned forward, opening my heart to the night.

A few of the publications of
THE NAIAD PRESS, INC.
P.O. Box 10543   •   Tallahassee, Florida 32302
Phone (904) 539-5965
Mail orders welcome. Please include 15% postage.

SOUTHBOUND by Sheila Ortiz Taylor. 240 pp. Hilarious sequel
to *Faultline.*   ISBN 0-941483-78-9 $8.95

SIDE BY SIDE by Isabel Miller. 256 pp. From beloved author of
Patience and Sarah.   ISBN 0-941483-77-0   8.95

STAYING POWER: LONG TERM LESBIAN COUPLES
by Susan E. Johnson. 352 pp. Joys of coupledom.
                                                     ISBN 0-941-483-75-4   12.95

SLICK by Camarin Grae. 304 pp. Exotic, erotic adventure.
                                                     ISBN 0-941483-74-6   9.95

NINTH LIFE by Lauren Wright Douglas. 256 pp. A Caitlin
Reece mystery. 2nd in a series.   ISBN 0-941483-50-9   8.95

PLAYERS by Robbi Sommers. 192 pp. Sizzling, erotic novel.
                                                     ISBN 0-941483-73-8   8.95

MURDER AT RED ROOK RANCH by Dorothy Tell. 224 pp.
First Poppy Dillworth adventure.   ISBN 0-941483-80-0   8.95

LESBIAN SURVIVAL MANUAL by Rhonda Dicksion.
112 pp. Cartoons!   ISBN 0-941483-71-1   8.95

A ROOM FULL OF WOMEN by Elisabeth Nonas. 256 pp.
Contemporary Lesbian lives.   ISBN 0-941483-69-X   8.95

MURDER IS RELATIVE by Karen Saum. 256 pp. The first
Brigid Donovan mystery.   ISBN 0-941483-70-3   8.95

PRIORITIES by Lynda Lyons 288 pp. Science fiction with a
twist.   ISBN 0-941483-66-5   8.95

THEME FOR DIVERSE INSTRUMENTS by Jane Rule.
208 pp. Powerful romantic lesbian stories.   ISBN 0-941483-63-0   8.95

LESBIAN QUERIES by Hertz & Ertman. 112 pp. The questions
you were too embarrassed to ask.   ISBN 0-941483-67-3   8.95

CLUB 12 by Amanda Kyle Williams. 288 pp. Espionage thriller
featuring a lesbian agent!   ISBN 0-941483-64-9   8.95

DEATH DOWN UNDER by Claire McNab. 240 pp. 3rd Det.
Insp. Carol Ashton mystery.   ISBN 0-941483-39-8   8.95

MONTANA FEATHERS by Penny Hayes. 256 pp. Vivian and
Elizabeth find love in frontier Montana.   ISBN 0-941483-61-4   8.95

CHESAPEAKE PROJECT by Phyllis Horn. 304 pp. Jessie &
Meredith in perilous adventure.   ISBN 0-941483-58-4   8.95

LIFESTYLES by Jackie Calhoun. 224 pp. Contemporary Lesbian lives and loves. ISBN 0-941483-57-6 8.95

VIRAGO by Karen Marie Christa Minns. 208 pp. Darsen has chosen Ginny. ISBN 0-941483-56-8 8.95

WILDERNESS TREK by Dorothy Tell. 192 pp. Six women on vacation learning "new" skills. ISBN 0-941483-60-6 8.95

MURDER BY THE BOOK by Pat Welch. 256 pp. A Helen Black Mystery. First in a series. ISBN 0-941483-59-2 8.95

BERRIGAN by Vicki P. McConnell. 176 pp. Youthful Lesbian– romantic, idealistic Berrigan. ISBN 0-941483-55-X 8.95

LESBIANS IN GERMANY by Lillian Faderman & B. Eriksson. 128 pp. Fiction, poetry, essays. ISBN 0-941483-62-2 8.95

THE BEVERLY MALIBU by Katherine V. Forrest. 288 pp. A Kate Delafield Mystery. 3rd in a series. ISBN 0-941483-47-9 16.95

THERE'S SOMETHING I'VE BEEN MEANING TO TELL YOU Ed. by Loralee MacPike. 288 pp. Gay men and lesbians coming out to their children. ISBN 0-941483-44-4 9.95
  ISBN 0-941483-54-1 16.95

LIFTING BELLY by Gertrude Stein. Ed. by Rebecca Mark. 104 pp. Erotic poetry. ISBN 0-941483-51-7 8.95
  ISBN 0-941483-53-3 14.95

ROSE PENSKI by Roz Perry. 192 pp. Adult lovers in a long-term relationship. ISBN 0-941483-37-1 8.95

AFTER THE FIRE by Jane Rule. 256 pp. Warm, human novel by this incomparable author. ISBN 0-941483-45-2 8.95

SUE SLATE, PRIVATE EYE by Lee Lynch. 176 pp. The gay folk of Peacock Alley are all cats. ISBN 0-941483-52-5 8.95

CHRIS by Randy Salem. 224 pp. Golden oldie. Handsome Chris and her adventures. ISBN 0-941483-42-8 8.95

THREE WOMEN by March Hastings. 232 pp. Golden oldie. A triangle among wealthy sophisticates. ISBN 0-941483-43-6 8.95

RICE AND BEANS by Valeria Taylor. 232 pp. Love and romance on poverty row. ISBN 0-941483-41-X 8.95

PLEASURES by Robbi Sommers. 204 pp. Unprecedented eroticism. ISBN 0-941483-49-5 8.95

EDGEWISE by Camarin Grae. 372 pp. Spellbinding adventure. ISBN 0-941483-19-3 9.95

FATAL REUNION by Claire McNab. 216 pp. 2nd Det. Inspec. Carol Ashton mystery. ISBN 0-941483-40-1 8.95

KEEP TO ME STRANGER by Sarah Aldridge. 372 pp. Romance set in a department store dynasty. ISBN 0-941483-38-X 9.95

HEARTSCAPE by Sue Gambill. 204 pp. American lesbian in Portugal. ISBN 0-941483-33-9   8.95

IN THE BLOOD by Lauren Wright Douglas. 252 pp. Lesbian science fiction adventure fantasy ISBN 0-941483-22-3   8.95

THE BEE'S KISS by Shirley Verel. 216 pp. Delicate, delicious romance. ISBN 0-941483-36-3   8.95

RAGING MOTHER MOUNTAIN by Pat Emmerson. 264 pp. Furosa Firechild's adventures in Wonderland. ISBN 0-941483-35-5   8.95

IN EVERY PORT by Karin Kallmaker. 228 pp. Jessica's sexy, adventuresome travels. ISBN 0-941483-37-7   8.95

OF LOVE AND GLORY by Evelyn Kennedy. 192 pp. Exciting WWII romance. ISBN 0-941483-32-0   8.95

CLICKING STONES by Nancy Tyler Glenn. 288 pp. Love transcending time. ISBN 0-941483-31-2   8.95

SURVIVING SISTERS by Gail Pass. 252 pp. Powerful love story. ISBN 0-941483-16-9   8.95

SOUTH OF THE LINE by Catherine Ennis. 216 pp. Civil War adventure. ISBN 0-941483-29-0   8.95

WOMAN PLUS WOMAN by Dolores Klaich. 300 pp. Supurb Lesbian overview. ISBN 0-941483-28-2   9.95

SLOW DANCING AT MISS POLLY'S by Sheila Ortiz Taylor. 96 pp. Lesbian Poetry ISBN 0-941483-30-4   7.95

DOUBLE DAUGHTER by Vicki P. McConnell. 216 pp. A Nyla Wade Mystery, third in the series. ISBN 0-941483-26-6   8.95

HEAVY GILT by Delores Klaich. 192 pp. Lesbian detective/ disappearing homophobes/upper class gay society.

ISBN 0-941483-25-8   8.95

THE FINER GRAIN by Denise Ohio. 216 pp. Brilliant young college lesbian novel. ISBN 0-941483-11-8   8.95

THE AMAZON TRAIL by Lee Lynch. 216 pp. Life, travel & lore of famous lesbian author. ISBN 0-941483-27-4   8.95

HIGH CONTRAST by Jessie Lattimore. 264 pp. Women of the Crystal Palace. ISBN 0-941483-17-7   8.95

OCTOBER OBSESSION by Meredith More. Josie's rich, secret Lesbian life. ISBN 0-941483-18-5   8.95

LESBIAN CROSSROADS by Ruth Baetz. 276 pp. Contemporary Lesbian lives. ISBN 0-941483-21-5   9.95

BEFORE STONEWALL: THE MAKING OF A GAY AND LESBIAN COMMUNITY by Andrea Weiss & Greta Schiller. 96 pp., 25 illus. ISBN 0-941483-20-7   7.95

WE WALK THE BACK OF THE TIGER by Patricia A. Murphy.
192 pp. Romantic Lesbian novel/beginning women's movement.
                                    ISBN 0-941483-13-4   8.95

SUNDAY'S CHILD by Joyce Bright. 216 pp. Lesbian athletics, at
last the novel about sports.   ISBN 0-941483-12-6   8.95

OSTEN'S BAY by Zenobia N. Vole. 204 pp. Sizzling adventure
romance set on Bonaire.   ISBN 0-941483-15-0   8.95

LESSONS IN MURDER by Claire McNab. 216 pp. 1st Det. Inspec.
Carol Ashton mystery — erotic tension!.   ISBN 0-941483-14-2   8.95

YELLOWTHROAT by Penny Hayes. 240 pp. Margarita, bandit,
kidnaps Julia.   ISBN 0-941483-10-X   8.95

SAPPHISTRY: THE BOOK OF LESBIAN SEXUALITY by
Pat Califia. 3d edition, revised. 208 pp.   ISBN 0-941483-24-X   8.95

CHERISHED LOVE by Evelyn Kennedy. 192 pp. Erotic
Lesbian love story.   ISBN 0-941483-08-8   8.95

LAST SEPTEMBER by Helen R. Hull. 208 pp. Six stories & a
glorious novella.   ISBN 0-941483-09-6   8.95

THE SECRET IN THE BIRD by Camarin Grae. 312 pp. Striking,
psychological suspense novel.   ISBN 0-941483-05-3   8.95

TO THE LIGHTNING by Catherine Ennis. 208 pp. Romantic
Lesbian 'Robinson Crusoe' adventure.   ISBN 0-941483-06-1   8.95

THE OTHER SIDE OF VENUS by Shirley Verel. 224 pp.
Luminous, romantic love story.   ISBN 0-941483-07-X   8.95

DREAMS AND SWORDS by Katherine V. Forrest. 192 pp.
Romantic, erotic, imaginative stories.   ISBN 0-941483-03-7   8.95

MEMORY BOARD by Jane Rule. 336 pp. Memorable novel
about an aging Lesbian couple.   ISBN 0-941483-02-9   9.95

THE ALWAYS ANONYMOUS BEAST by Lauren Wright
Douglas. 224 pp. A Caitlin Reece mystery. First in a series.
                                    ISBN 0-941483-04-5   8.95

SEARCHING FOR SPRING by Patricia A. Murphy. 224 pp.
Novel about the recovery of love.   ISBN 0-941483-00-2   8.95

DUSTY'S QUEEN OF HEARTS DINER by Lee Lynch. 240 pp.
Romantic blue-collar novel.   ISBN 0-941483-01-0   8.95

PARENTS MATTER by Ann Muller. 240 pp. Parents'
relationships with Lesbian daughters and gay sons.
                                    ISBN 0-930044-91-6   9.95

THE PEARLS by Shelley Smith. 176 pp. Passion and fun in
the Caribbean sun.   ISBN 0-930044-93-2   7.95

MAGDALENA by Sarah Aldridge. 352 pp. Epic Lesbian novel
set on three continents.   ISBN 0-930044-99-1   8.95

THE BLACK AND WHITE OF IT by Ann Allen Shockley.
144 pp. Short stories.   ISBN 0-930044-96-7   7.95

SAY JESUS AND COME TO ME by Ann Allen Shockley. 288
pp. Contemporary romance.   ISBN 0-930044-98-3   8.95

LOVING HER by Ann Allen Shockley. 192 pp. Romantic love
story.   ISBN 0-930044-97-5   7.95

MURDER AT THE NIGHTWOOD BAR by Katherine V.
Forrest. 240 pp. A Kate Delafield mystery. Second in a series.
                                          ISBN 0-930044-92-4   8.95

ZOE'S BOOK by Gail Pass. 224 pp. Passionate, obsessive love
story.   ISBN 0-930044-95-9   7.95

WINGED DANCER by Camarin Grae. 228 pp. Erotic Lesbian
adventure story.   ISBN 0-930044-88-6   8.95

PAZ by Camarin Grae. 336 pp. Romantic Lesbian adventurer
with the power to change the world.   ISBN 0-930044-89-4   8.95

SOUL SNATCHER by Camarin Grae. 224 pp. A puzzle, an
adventure, a mystery — Lesbian romance.   ISBN 0-930044-90-8   8.95

THE LOVE OF GOOD WOMEN by Isabel Miller. 224 pp.
Long-awaited new novel by the author of the beloved *Patience
and Sarah*.   ISBN 0-930044-81-9   8.95

THE HOUSE AT PELHAM FALLS by Brenda Weathers. 240
pp. Suspenseful Lesbian ghost story.   ISBN 0-930044-79-7   7.95

HOME IN YOUR HANDS by Lee Lynch. 240 pp. More stories
from the author of *Old Dyke Tales*.   ISBN 0-930044-80-0   7.95

EACH HAND A MAP by Anita Skeen. 112 pp. Real-life poems
that touch us all.   ISBN 0-930044-82-7   6.95

SURPLUS by Sylvia Stevenson. 342 pp. A classic early Lesbian
novel.   ISBN 0-930044-78-9   7.95

PEMBROKE PARK by Michelle Martin. 256 pp. Derring-do
and daring romance in Regency England.   ISBN 0-930044-77-0   7.95

THE LONG TRAIL by Penny Hayes. 248 pp. Vivid adventures
of two women in love in the old west.   ISBN 0-930044-76-2   8.95

HORIZON OF THE HEART by Shelley Smith. 192 pp. Hot
romance in summertime New England.   ISBN 0-930044-75-4   7.95

AN EMERGENCE OF GREEN by Katherine V. Forrest. 288
pp. Powerful novel of sexual discovery.   ISBN 0-930044-69-X   8.95

THE LESBIAN PERIODICALS INDEX edited by Claire
Potter. 432 pp. Author & subject index.   ISBN 0-930044-74-6   29.95

DESERT OF THE HEART by Jane Rule. 224 pp. A classic;
basis for the movie *Desert Hearts*.   ISBN 0-930044-73-8   8.95

SPRING FORWARD/FALL BACK by Sheila Ortiz Taylor.
288 pp. Literary novel of timeless love. ISBN 0-930044-70-3   7.95

FOR KEEPS by Elisabeth Nonas. 144 pp. Contemporary novel
about losing and finding love.   ISBN 0-930044-71-1   7.95

TORCHLIGHT TO VALHALLA by Gale Wilhelm. 128 pp.
Classic novel by a great Lesbian writer.   ISBN 0-930044-68-1   7.95

LESBIAN NUNS: BREAKING SILENCE edited by Rosemary
Curb and Nancy Manahan. 432 pp. Unprecedented autobiographies
of religious life.   ISBN 0-930044-62-2   9.95

THE SWASHBUCKLER by Lee Lynch. 288 pp. Colorful novel
set in Greenwich Village in the sixties.   ISBN 0-930044-66-5   8.95

MISFORTUNE'S FRIEND by Sarah Aldridge. 320 pp. Histori-
cal Lesbian novel set on two continents.   ISBN 0-930044-67-3   7.95

A STUDIO OF ONE'S OWN by Ann Stokes. Edited by
Dolores Klaich. 128 pp. Autobiography.   ISBN 0-930044-64-9   7.95

SEX VARIANT WOMEN IN LITERATURE by Jeannette
Howard Foster. 448 pp. Literary history.   ISBN 0-930044-65-7   8.95

A HOT-EYED MODERATE by Jane Rule. 252 pp. Hard-hitting
essays on gay life; writing; art.   ISBN 0-930044-57-6   7.95

INLAND PASSAGE AND OTHER STORIES by Jane Rule.
288 pp. Wide-ranging new collection.   ISBN 0-930044-56-8   7.95

WE TOO ARE DRIFTING by Gale Wilhelm. 128 pp. Timeless
Lesbian novel, a masterpiece.   ISBN 0-930044-61-4   6.95

AMATEUR CITY by Katherine V. Forrest. 224 pp. A Kate
Delafield mystery. First in a series.   ISBN 0-930044-55-X   8.95

THE SOPHIE HOROWITZ STORY by Sarah Schulman. 176
pp. Engaging novel of madcap intrigue.   ISBN 0-930044-54-1   7.95

THE BURNTON WIDOWS by Vickie P. McConnell. 272 pp. A
Nyla Wade mystery, second in the series.   ISBN 0-930044-52-5   7.95

OLD DYKE TALES by Lee Lynch. 224 pp. Extraordinary
stories of our diverse Lesbian lives.   ISBN 0-930044-51-7   8.95

DAUGHTERS OF A CORAL DAWN by Katherine V. Forrest.
240 pp. Novel set in a Lesbian new world.   ISBN 0-930044-50-9   8.95

THE PRICE OF SALT by Claire Morgan. 288 pp. A milestone
novel, a beloved classic.   ISBN 0-930044-49-5   8.95

AGAINST THE SEASON by Jane Rule. 224 pp. Luminous,
complex novel of interrelationships.   ISBN 0-930044-48-7   8.95

These are just a few of the many Naiad Press titles — we are the oldest and
largest lesbian/feminist publishing company in the world. Please request a
complete catalog. We offer personal service; we encourage and welcome
direct mail orders from individuals who have limited access to bookstores
carrying our publications.